William Cunningham Gray

Life of Abraham Lincoln

William Cunningham Gray

Life of Abraham Lincoln

ISBN/EAN: 9783337332716

Printed in Europe, USA, Canada, Australia, Japan

Cover: Foto ©Raphael Reischuk / pixelio.de

More available books at **www.hansebooks.com**

Abraham Lincoln.

FOR THE YOUNG MAN AND THE SABBATH SCHOOL.

By WM. C. GRAY.

"Having chosen our course without guile and with pure purpose, let us renew our trust in God, and go on without fear and with manly hearts."—*Message, July 5, 1861.*

CINCINNATI:

WESTERN TRACT AND BOOK SOCIETY,

No. 28 West Fourth Street.

1867.

STEREOTYPED AT THE
FRANKLIN TYPE FOUNDRY,
CINCINNATI.

CONTENTS.

(iii)

iv CONTENTS.

PREFACE.

—◇◇—

THE emancipation of four millions of people from a state of bondage, the most cruel and degrading known in the annals of oppression, was an event which will fix attention so long as history shall be read. The prominence attained by the Chief Magis-. trate who led in the achievement of this grand result, and the affection cherished for him by the people whose liberties he so greatly aided in preserving, combine to render his personal example a moral power with the masses. To the colored race he stands in a higher relationship than that of any man who ever lived. Crushed for half a thousand years in a bondage which seemed as hopeless as it was cruel, the light of liberty burst upon them with a suddenness that brought shouts of wildest joy from every lip; and Abraham Lincoln became to them the Angel of Deliverance, sent direct on his mission by the blessed Jesus. Their enthusiastic gratitude kindled almost to idolatry. "He walks de earf like de Lord," exclaimed an aged freedman in describing the Emancipator. With these people the example of honesty, industry, and humanity found in Abraham Lincoln will have an influence proportionate to the love and veneration in which his memory is held.

(v)

The design of this volume is to portray the life and character of this honored patriot in a volume the brevity of which will render it available for wide circulation in home circles and Sabbath-schools, and among that grateful and affectionate people who have most reason to cherish and honor his memory.

While the central object in view in writing these pages was the commendation of pure Christian morality, the facts and attending circumstances of Lincoln's life produce also an argument of a different cast and higher range. However nakedly stated, and for whatever purpose, they illuminate the truth of the discriminating, particular, and unerring PROVIDENCE OF GOD, with a brightness that has fastened the attention of the Christian world.

The palm of martyrdom gives peculiar fragrance to the fame of any champion of the right. This is particularly true of one whose name had already been enshrined in the affections of the people. While writing under these influences, we have sought to avoid a spirit of hero-worship; to represent and commend that which is admirable and worthy of imitation, and to condemn with impartiality that which may be used in apology for evil.   W. O. G.

ABRAHAM LINCOLN.

CHAPTER I.

PARENTAGE AND CHILDHOOD.

BRAHAM LINCOLN was born on Nolin Creek, in Hardin County, Kentucky, on the 12th of February, 1809. Before that time, the savage tribes had been defeated and driven from his native State, but they yet lingered in broken and straggling bands in the adjacent territory, north and south, and reigned in their original power a few leagues westward. The whole country west of the Kanawha was, as yet, a wilderness, almost undisturbed. The great forests covered the solitary hills and valleys. The deer and bears had not yet forsaken their ancient haunts. The dashing

(7)

saw-mills had not riven to planks the giant oaks and poplars. No busy grist-mills, driven by the tumbling waterfall, prepared the settler's corn. The swift locomotive, with its shrill shriek, was a thing as unknown to little Abe as it was to Abraham of old, sitting by his tent on the field of Mamre. Some shreds or antiquated garments of silk or broadcloth may have descended from the past as family mementoes, but otherwise they were unknown. The free school and the Sabbath school, with their precious privileges and delightful surroundings, were in reserve for the children of a later day. "Home" was a word as sweet to the heart then as now, but little Abe's home and those of his neighbors were not such as the most of children now enjoy. Little cabins of rough logs and clay, covered with clapboards, floored with puncheons, beds often of leaves, a fire-place nearly as wide and deep as a bed is long and broad—such was "home," and yet little Abe's father and mother devoutly thanked God for the protection and comfort it afforded them; and well they should, for even such a home was a great blessing.

Their fare consisted of corn-bread, milk, and such luxuries as the garden, field, and woods

afforded them. It was abundant—often luxu-
rious. The wild plum, blackberry, raspberry,
fox-grape and other fruits grew in rich profu-
sion; while squirrels, venison, and fat turkeys
were to be had by the sharp-shooting pioneers,
for the taking. The maple gave freely the most
delicious sweet that nature anywhere affords.
The gold of a king could purchase nothing nicer
than the sugar fresh and warm from the kettle.
And then how pleasant it was to sit in a cozy
camp before the roaring furnace, gaze at the
stars through the swaying branches above, listen
to the music of the dripping "spiles," and dream
of the future, as many a ragged backwoods boy
has done. Hickory-nuts rattled down in plenty
on the yellow leaves—little Abe probably knew
all the best trees for a mile around—and many
were the pleasant winter nights spent till bedtime
around the great "fire-place" cracking them and
telling Indian and bear stories while the icy
winds were tossing the snow drifts without.

Little is known of his ancestry, and that little
does not extend far back into the past. His
grandfather came to Kentucky, from Virginia,
in 1780, or eleven years after the famous pioneer,
Daniel Boone, first established his cabin on Ken-

tucky soil. He brought a large family of little
children to brave the dangers and privations of
pioneer life, but he lived only four years to afford
them protection and support. While working in
the woods one day a skulking savage stole upon
him and shot him dead. We may imagine the
terror and distress which fell upon the wife and
little ones at this dreadful calamity; and yet it
was not the helpless despair which would have
seized upon a family of our times could they have
been placed in similar circumstances. Such oc-
currences were not then uncommon. Pioneer's
wives were brave spirited and adequate to such
emergencies. Not long before this occurrence,
and in the same county, lived a settler and his
family named Davis. The husband was absent
from home one day, and his wife, with the sharp
scrutiny, which exposure to danger had given,
observed an Indian peering from behind the door
of the stable, about ten rods distant from the
cabin. She well knew his hostile intent, but did
not scream, or faint, or do any such like absurd
thing. Walking carelessly into her cabin, she
took down her husband's rifle, crept into the loft,
carefully placed the muzzle in a crevice between
the logs, aimed long and well, and fired. With a

yell of rage and pain the savage broke from his covert and fled to the woods, his speed hastened by a defiant cheer from the undaunted woman. Many such instances of hardihood and bravery, and not a few of high moral heroism might be given of the pioneer women of those early times.

The part of the country where the grandfather Lincoln was killed is not known. The widow gathered up her children and removed to Washington County, then more thickly settled—if such an expression may be used in reference to an exceedingly sparce population—and there reared, as best she could, the little ones cast wholly upon her care. The father of Abraham Lincoln grew up an ignorant, wandering boy. He could not so much as read, but was respected as a man of inflexible honesty and generous nature, and beloved for his amiability and kindness. Abraham's mother came from Virginia. She was a woman of elevated Christian character, posessing sound judgment and strong common sense. With these traits in an eminent degree, she was humble, tender, and loving. What a precious mother was that for a little boy! How sweet her memory. Mr. Lincoln always looked back to her, amid the storms of political strife and furious war, with deepest reverence and affection. "All that I am or hope to be," he said, "I owe to my angel mother—blessings on her memory." It is much to have such a mother on earth, much to have such a mother in heaven to draw our affections to that blessed place, and to meet us when Jesus shall have redeemed us and called us to himself. Let us who are so blessed thank God every day for a pious mother, whether she be on earth or in heaven.

There was no church or school within many miles of the humble home of this little family. Abraham had a little sister whom he tenderly loved, and a little brother who died young. The well-worn Bible and the family circle were almost the only means of religious instruction afforded to these children. An itinerant Baptist minister, Parson Elkin, came at intervals of many months and held public worship at some of the settlers' cabins, or beneath the spreading branches of a forest tree, and to his rude but earnest eloquence the little family and their neighbors listened with pleasure and profit. Those early pioneer preachers, in their simplicity and devotion, remind us of the saints of olden time, "who wandered about in sheep-

skins and goat-skins destitute and afflicted."
They rode through forests and wilds, swam
rivers, and braved the tempests for the love of
Jesus. They thought little of their hardships,
and God was with them. God always goes with
his children who love him. An old itenerant,
with white locks, relates the following incident
of those times. He was walking across a wide
prairie. Night came upon him, and foot-sore
and weary, he sought a place to rest. Finding
a little tree he lay down and placed his feet up
against it, as they ached less while raised higher
than his body. He heard the wolves howling in
the distance and was greatly afraid. However,
he prayed and fell asleep. As soon as he slept
he dreamed he saw a bright angel standing over
him with a drawn and glittering sword, who said,
"Sleep without fear, I have come to protect
you." The morning sun awoke the minister
from a refreshing sleep, and he went on his way
with a psalm of joy.

The opportunities for education were quite
as limited. At the age of seven Abraham was
sent to school for about two months. The school
was kept in a vacant cabin by a catholic school-
master named Zachariah Riney. A school-

teacher he could scarcely be called. "Zack" was as innocent" of any knowledge of geography or grammar as little bare-footed Abe himself. But the young pupil rapidly mastered the mysteries of his borrowed speller, and took care, when the school closed, not to forget what he had learned. The next year he had another opportunity of attending a school kept by a young man named Caleb Hazel. At the end of Hazel's "quarter" little Abe could both read and write pretty well. For several years afterward his penmanship was cultivated by writing with coals upon the smooth end of chopped logs, and his reading by lessons in the Bible and a copy of Pilgrim's Progress, which, taken together, constituted the "family library." His time was busily employed in wielding the ax and hoe, clearing fields, building fence, and such other rugged labors as he had strength to perform.

These were hardships, and yet how much of genuine boyish pleasure was mingled with them. For instance, what grand sport it was to fire the brush-heaps at night! How the flames leaped and crackled, the great trees suddenly standing out from the darkness with shadows swaying like phantoms in a dream. And then to see the dry trees in the "deadening" wrapped in twisting fire, or tumbling with a crash in clouds of sparks and smoke. Those were better bon-fires than those made of store-boxes and barrels, lighted for a better purpose, and free from evil surroundings.

CHAPTER II.

THE FIRST REMOVAL.

WHEN Abraham was ten years old, his father sold his farm for ten barrels of whisky and twenty dollars in money. Leaving his family at home, he took his whisky and a few farming utensils, on an ox-wagon, and started to find and prepare a new abode in the dark woods of Indiana. . Arriving at the Ohio River, he attempted to cross it, with his valuables, in a flat-boat. Unfortunately—fortunately, we would say of a similar occurrence in our times— one of the barrels slipped from its place, upsetting the boat and tumbling whisky, plows, and boatman into the river. He saved but little of his property, and considered himself fortunate to have escaped with his life.

It must not be supposed that Mr. Lincoln was an immoral man because he received whisky in part pay for his farm. The terrible conse-

quences of intemperance were not so prominent
in the thinly populated country as they afterward became, and public opinion was not then
enlightened on this subject. Whisky was a common beverage among all classes, rich and poor,
ministers and people. Little log distilleries were
found in every neighborhood, and the whisky-jug
in almost every house. If such customs prevailed now the consequences would be indescriba-
bly destructive of morals, life, and property.

Having selected a home in Spencer County,
Indiana, he returned for his family, and they were
soon housed in a new cabin. The little furniture
which they had was in the river. To begin with,
a bed must be had; they had no bedstead, and
no means of getting one but to make it, and no
tools but the augur and ax to make it with. But
the process was simple. A stake was driven in
the ground near the corner of the cabin, about
four feet from one wall and six from the other;
augur-holes were then bored in the logs opposite,
and poles driven into them, the other ends meeting on the stake. Across these were laid laths,
rived from an oak log, and upon them rested the
straw bed. A little three-legged stool, also the
result of saw-and-ax carpentry, was the incipient

2

presidential chair. A fire-place, nearly as wide as the end of the cabin, built of logs, and lined with broad stones and clay, a few shelves, a puncheon table, and such like conveniences, completed the establishment.

Shortly after the family were settled in their new quarters, little Abe distinguished himself by a noted feat with his father's rifle, which always hung upon a pair of wooden hooks above the fire-place. His father was out chopping, and his mother and little sister engaged in firing brush-heaps, when Abe heard the call of a flock of wild turkeys in the woods at the back of the house. Mounting his stool, he reached the rifle down with trembling hands, put the muzzle out of a crevice, and gave the adventurous gobblers a broadside. One of them sprang high in the air, and came down flapping and fanning up the dry leaves in its last flutter. Dropping his gun, he ran out with a whoop of triumph, and bore his game aloft to his admiring little sister and mother. Game was abundant—in fact the only reliance of the pioneers for meat—and doubtless little Abe, with his father, often followed the bay of the trusty "coon-dog, in the darkness and stillness of the heavy forests; yet he never afterward so greatly

distinguished himself as a hunter as on the famous day when he brought down his first gob-
bler.

But a dark day was at hand for the little pioneer family. The devoted, tender wife and
mother was seized with a quick consumption,
and almost before the desolate family could realize it she was gone to her Savior. With many
a bitter tear and despairing sob, they prepared
a grave near the cabin and laid her to rest.

So passed away from an humble cabin home a
woman who had done more to elevate and bless
the human race than the greatest empress that
ever wore a crown. The principles of justice,
the love of truth, which she had implanted in
the heart of her little boy, and the kindly, patient, persevering nature which he inherited from
her, made him the great liberator of a prostrate
race.

Little Abe sat down, in his grief, and wrote to
Parson Elkin, who lived near the old Lincoln
home in Kentucky, requesting him to come and
preach a funeral sermon at the grave of his
mother. In due time an answer came, appoint-
ing a day when the parson would preach. He
traveled over one hundred miles on horseback

to pay the last honors to one whose godliness
and worth he had so well known. Word had
been passed from house to house, and on the
appointed day a congregation of about two hundred people assembled, some of them coming
a distance of twenty miles. At the foot of the
grave, and surrounded by that congregation of
coarsely-clad but earnest worshipers, the minister lifted his voice in the solemn hymn, the simple prayer, and the plain-spoken but eloquent
appeals of the Gospel.

About two years afterward the father married
a Mrs. Sarah Johnston, who lived near their old
home in Kentucky. She proved to be an amiable and provident step-mother.

CHAPTER III.

LIFE IN INDIANA.

THE inconveniences and privations of their life in Indiana is shown by the fact that there was no grist-mill nearer than fifty miles distant from their home, and that was a rude affair, in which the grinding-stones were slowly turned by a horse hitched at the end of a lever. Meal was usually manufactured in a large wooden mortar, formed by burning a bowl into the end of a log of oak or other hard wood. The corn was beaten in this with a heavy wooden pestle, suspended by bending over a tough sappling and tying the pestle to it with a piece of leather. This saved labor by lifting the pestle after it had been brought down with all the operator's force upon the corn.

When Abraham was about fourteen years old he went occasionally to the horse-mill, ground his corn and returned, the whole trip occupying from four to five days. On one occasion, while grinding at this mill and following the horse in his rounds, the vicious animal gave him a severe kick, knocking him senseless. When he became conscious, he proceeded without delay to finish his grinding and return home.

About the same time, a man named Andrew Crawford, a neighboring farmer, opened a winter school on his own place. This school Abraham attended for about three months, and there learned the rudiments of arithmetic. Grammar was a mysterious science to most of the back-woods school-masters. An illustration of this occurred, at the same period, in a neighboring county in Ohio. John Woods, who afterward became a member of Congress, and a man of note and usefulness, having cyphered as far as the "Single Rule of Three," heard of a teacher some miles off who "knew grammar," and forth-with posted away to attend his school. He became so absorbed in the study that he was ac-customed to con over his lesson on the way to and from school. One evening his father and the family were startled by their trusty neigh-bor, Deacon Silvers, who rode up to the house in hot haste, and called out:

"I say, Alex. Woods, your John is in the edge of my clearing, a mile back, sitting on a log, and he's crazy as a loon! Come, and I'll help you home with him afore he gits away."

"What's that ye say?" exclaimed the astonished father; "ye don't mean to say"—

"I say he's gone crazy, and I'm afeard he'll be off into the woods, and may be die there."

"And what's he at that makes ye think so?" excitedly asked the mother, while "Alex." was after his hat.

"He's talking gibberish and staring at the ground. He says 'I love, you love, she loves; nom'tive I possesses me.' He's mad crazy; and Mrs. Woods, I believe it was that Jane Pettigrew that cracked the silly fellow's head—I'm very sorry for you, Mrs. Woods."

The acquaintance of Abraham with Mr. Crawford, as pupil and teacher, resulted in mutual confidence and esteem. Mr. Crawford had in his possession an old copy of Weems's life of Washington, which Abe greatly desired to read, and Mr. Crawford freely loaned it to him. He pored delighted over the history of that great and good man by whose side he was destined to stand in the pages of history and in the affections of mankind. One unguarded evening he left it on a table near an open window. A dashing rain-storm blew up in the night, and the book was soaked through and ruined. Little Abe's grief and self-reproach knew no bounds at the discovery of this disaster. But he took up the book and went straight to the owner, showed him its condition, and offered to make payment in full. Mr. Crawford put him to the test by offering to take two days' corn-husking in payment for the loss. Abe regarded the proposal as very liberal, and at daylight next day was in the corn-field, and continued faithfully and industriously at the work till his obligation was discharged.

As Abraham grew up he became a muscular and powerful youth; but his strong arm and hard hand were never employed in bullying or oppressing his weaker companions. He loved peace and justice, and lacked neither courage nor will to enforce their observance when occasion required. Two stout and well-matched young rowdies, whom he had often reproved for their quarrelsome and profane conduct, getting into a fisticuff encounter at a log-rolling, he seized them both, dragged them to a pond close by, with

the intention of pitching them in, as he said, " to
cool them off," and was only dissuaded from
ducking them by their promises to behave more
decently in the future.

At another time, as he was going home one
freezing winter night with two companions, from
a debating society, they found an incorrigible
toper, well known in the neighborhood, lying
drunk upon the snow. His companions proposed
to let him lie there, as he was worthless and past
reformation. Not so, thought Abraham. If he
was a miserable sot he was still a *man*, and he
would not willingly let him pass from his inebriate
sleep into the sleep of death, to wake in a dread
eternity. He asked his companions to aid him by
lifting the half-lifeless form from the snow, while
he sank upon one knee to receive it. Having the
drunken man balanced across his shoulder, he
rose and carried him a distance of a quarter of
a mile, to the nearest house, and stayed with
him till morning, sparing no efforts to save his
life. The drunkard lived, but so great was the
power of appetite that the terrible lesson of that
night was lost upon him, and he soon after filled
a drunkard's grave.

Alcohol is one of the most deceptive and

deadly enemies of the human race. It besets
the young man in many attractive forms, and
disguises itself in generous virtues. It stills his
fears, hushes conscience, and leads him in giddy
mazes of delirium to that

> ——mysterious bourne
> By which our path is crossed,
> Beyond which God himself hath sworn
> That he who goes is lost.

CHAPTER IV.

FIRST VOYAGE TO NEW ORLEANS.

AT the age of eighteen, Abraham longed to see more of the great world than his secluded life had yet brought to his view. A pleasure trip by post-roads and public conveyances was out of the question. But combining toil with pleasure, with the assistance of a few neighbors, he built a little flat-boat, launched it on the Ohio, loaded it with such produce as his neighbors were willing to risk in the adventure, and with one companion, pushed off to find the far-distant market at New Orleans. While he was preparing to start, a little occurrence took place, which, insignificant as it seems, produced a marked impression on his mind. As he stood at the landing loading his boat, two passengers came up, who wished to be placed on an approaching steamer. Abe volunteered, and having safely placed them on board and handed up their baggage, they each threw back into the bottom of his canoe a silver half dollar. "I could scarcely believe my eyes," said the President afterward, in relating this incident, "I could scarcely believe that I, a poor boy, had earned a dollar in less than a day. The world seemed wider and fairer to me. I was a more hopeful and confident being from that time."

The vast extent and power of our country must have been strongly impressed upon his mind by that voyage of eighteen hundred miles. Floating slowly down for days and weeks upon the mighty rivers, the hills and rocks, prairies and forests, with ever-varying scenery, which rose upon his vision, were all new, vast, and strange to him as they were to Marquette, whose canoe, first of any white explorer, traversed those great rivers. He and his companion alternately slept in a little bunk on the deck, keeping watch at night when there was light enough to keep the boat off the bars and snags, and approaching the shore when it was necessary to cook their simple meals of mush and venison, or rashers of pork.

Arriving at a little town below Natchez, Abe had his first acquaintance with some of the features of slavery. During the night, when he and his companion were asleep, seven stout negro slaves, in quest of more liberal rations than the negro quarters afforded them, undertook to rob the boat. Abe suddenly awoke before they had succeeded in boarding his deck, and, seizing a handspike, knocked four of them off the plank into the water. The other three fled, but Abe's blood was up, and he and his companion pursued and administered a severe pounding to each of them. The next castigation he inflicted in that "sunny land" was on a much larger scale, and the subjects of it were robbers of loftiest pretentions.

Having disposed of his cargo and the boat which contained it, he returned home on foot— a weary journey of weeks.

The family had attained to years of maturity. Sarah Lincoln, Abraham's only sister, married a man named Aaron Grigsby, and about a year afterward died. His two step-sisters also married. The hard labor of clearing away the heavy timber to convert the land into productive fields was discouraging to the young people; and in addition to this, they suffered much from that obstinate and enervating affliction the fever and ague. Hearing much of the wide and fertile prairies of Illinois, they longed to find more pleasant homes and a more tractable soil from which to win their bread. The matter was discussed around the parental hearth many an evening during the winter of 1830, and they concluded to abandon the wooded hills for the far-famed prairies in the following spring. On the 30th of March they all, sons, daughters, husbands, and little ones, with their effects, loaded in ox-wagons, started on their westward way. The streams were swollen, the roads deep with mud, and the progress consequently slow and wearisome. After fifteen days' journeying, they rested on the north side of the Sangamon River, in Mason County, Illinois, about twelve miles west of Decatur. Abraham Lincoln entered Illinois on foot, in a threadbare suit of walnut jeans, splashed and smeared with mud, driving an ox-wagon; he left it the trusted President of his country, honoring the office more than it honored him.

Again the work of constructing a cabin was to be done; and in a few days one was built on a ridge which divided the woodland from the prairie—mostly the result of the stout arms of

ABRAHAM LINCOLN ENTERING ILLINOIS.

Abraham. He then set to work and split rails enough to fence ten acres, plowed and planted it before the first of June; and, having thus provided for his father's family, set out to seek his own fortune.

He was sadly in need of sufficient clothing to cover his lank but muscular limbs, and the first necessity was to provide himself a new suit. A widow named Mrs. Nancy Miller had a loom and plenty of flax and wool. Abe opened negotiations with her on the subject of his necessities, and concluded a bargain to chop and split twenty-nine hundred good rails for a suit of jeans, to be spun, woven, and made to fit. The widow and the axman each performed their part of the contract, and Mr. Lincoln rejoiced in a substantial suit of new clothes, shirt included.

Their old enemy, the fever and ague, again visited the Lincoln family, and the following spring they again abandoned their homes, this time removing to Coles County. Here Abraham worked about among the farmers, at such labor as he could get, for two years. It is related that a respectable-looking traveler stopped one evening at a farm-house where he was working, and requested a lodgment for the night. The host

informed him that he was welcome, but that
they had no spare bed, and that he would be
obliged to sleep with his hired man. "Let me
see him," said the gentleman. He was conducted around the house to where Abe lay, rest-
ing over six feet of himself upon the grass.
"He'll do," said the traveler, and so stayed
and slept with his future President.

Abraham's faithfulness and honesty were soon
known among his new acquaintances; also that
he had held the "responsible position" of captain of a flat-boat. A Kentucky trader, Denton
Offut, wishing to send a boat to New Orleans,
applied to him to undertake the trip. John
Hanks, a cousin of Abraham's mother, and a
stout young man named Johnston, were employed to accompany him. The trip was suc-
cessfully made, and the proceeds paid off to
Offut with scrupulous honesty.

At the period of Mr. Lincoln's life when he
became of age, there was nothing in his personal
appearance that would recommend him as a dry-
goods clerk, or indicate his probable success as
a merchant. Six feet four inches high, clad in
a blue warmus, with tow pantaloons a world too
short, coarse cowskin shoes, lank arms, a weather-

brown, angular face—the last man to twirl a yardstick, skip a counter, or play the agreeable to ladies—yet such was to be his next occupation. Offutt had a store in New Salem, of which the stock in trade consisted of an assortment of trace-chains, tea, sickles, sugar, mop-sticks, molasses, cheese, castor-oil, cotton lace, nails, ribbons, and similar goods, not forgetting a barrel of tar and one of vinegar in the cellar. His clerks had cheated and stolen from him to the extent that he was on the point of abandoning the business, but he concluded to make a trial of Abraham. He justified the confidence of his employer, and proved himself adequate to the business.

The honesty of Abraham Lincoln was exhibited in numerous instances while in the employ of Offutt, in matters which would seem to a person less conscientious to be trivial and unnecessary. Once he sold a woman a little bill of goods amounting, as he reckoned it, to two dollars and a sixpence. She paid the amount and left the store. Abe ran over the figures again to see that all was right, and discovered that he had charged her six and a quarter cents too much. It was night and dark, and the woman

3

lived nearly three miles away; but he closed the store, followed her home, and paid over the sixpence. Such exhibitions of rigid honesty show that he regarded strict adherence *to principle* as important in the smallest transactions. It was not a cunning attempt to secure a reputation for fair dealing and accuracy, for that would itself be dishonest, and wholly repugnant to his character. Most young men, in similar circumstances, would have quieted conscience by the reflection that the wrong was not intentional, and could be rectified at another time. His conduct shows that he did not consider this *procrastination* as honest. In this he was correct. Postponement is the first and fatal step in the total abandonment of duty.

This scrupulous regard for truth and justice was not confined to the rights of others. He was mild, patient, amiable, forgiving, but would not permit himself to be injured or humiliated without earnest and usually effective protest. He was a peace man but not a non-combatant. A number of illustrations of this trait occurred during his life, before he gave that grand display of heroism, endurance, and persistence which resulted in the defeat and destruction of slavery.

While in Offutt's store, an amusing test of his peculiar courage occurred. A swaggering bully and fighter came in while he was dealing with some ladies, and opened upon him with a torrent of vile and abusive language. Lincoln begged him to desist till the ladies were gone, when he would hear whatever he had to say. When the ladies had departed, the ruffian became more abusive and profane than ever. Abe listened to him a moment, and then said, in a reluctant way, " Well, I see that somebody will have to whip you, and I suppose I may as well do it as to leave the job for some other man."

Leaping over the counter, he walked out, followed by the pugilist, who stripped for the battle, while he poured out his most frightful threats and imprecations. Abe stood by, looking on, neither angry nor alarmed, but interested in this violent exhibition of *human nature*. The bully leaped from the ground, struck a scientific attitude, and declared himself READY. Lincoln seized him with the grip of a vice, threw him upon the grass, and, gathering a bunch of smart-weed, which grew at his feet, he rubbed it in the fellow's eyes till he bellowed with pain and begged for mercy; then lifting

him up, he led him to the well, furnished him
with a basin of water, "hoped it would not
smart long," and did what he could to afford
him relief.

His opportunities for acquiring knowledge,
meager as they might seem, were greatly increased by his employment in the store. While
there, a copy of Kirkham's Grammar fell into
his hands, and the common-sense method of
the old author led him easily and pleasantly, as
it did thousands of others, into the principles
of language. The author's plan of reasoning on
the subject, and his pithy attacks on the absurd-
ities of his predecessors, was the very style to
interest and delight the logic-loving mind of
Lincoln.

After Abraham had been in Offutt's employ a
little over a year, that gentleman failed in business; the store was closed, and Abe had to look
elsewhere for labor of muscle or brain. His
management of Offutt's business had gained him
the title of "Honest Abe," and the homely
phrase clung to him long after he had exhibited
much more striking and brilliant traits of mind
and character.

CHAPTER V.

THE INDIAN WAR.

IN 1831, while Abraham Lincoln was employed as a clerk, rumors of trouble with the Indians became prevalent throughout the Western States. In pursuance of a treaty made with them in 1825, they had retired from Illinois to the west of the Mississippi. The territory now included in the beautiful States of Iowa, Wisconsin, and Minnesota, and inhabited by a population second to none in the world in enterprise, intelligence, and patriotism, was then the country of warlike and powerful savage tribes. The Sacs and Foxes, Kickapoos, and Pottawatamies, in Iowa, and the Winnebagoes, Ottawas, and Chippewas in what is now Wisconsin and Minnesota, were as numerous as their kindred ever were in Kentucky or Ohio. It is astonishing to reflect that in one brief generation, thirty-five years only, they have so nearly disappeared and become extinct. But so it is or-

dained of Providence. Man may so degrade himself that the influences of civilization and light,
which to others are elevating, will be to him
harbingers of swift destruction. So it is with the
Gospel, the good news of Jesus Christ, our Savior—to some a message of joy and endless pro-
gression in happiness, to others a savor of death.

The famous Tecumseh and Black Hawk, old
chiefs of the Sacs, resolved to violate the treaty
and invade Illinois. This they did in the spring
of 1831; but on the approach of a few hundred
troops, under Gen. Gaines, retired to their own
territory. In 1832 they again crossed the river,
and Gov. Reynolds, of Illinois, called for volunteers to repel them, and Abraham, then twenty-
three years old, instantly responded, and, bor-
rowing a buck-rifle, repaired to the rendezvous
at Salem. His friends and neighbors—among
whom, and most zealous for him of all, was his
friend of the smart-weed combat—proposed him
for captain. A well-to-do and somewhat self-
important man, named Kirkpatrick, for whom
Abe had labored as a farm-hand, was seeking
and expecting the commission. An election was
held, and Abe beat his former employer by a
vote nearly unanimous.

The forces then assembled at Bardstown, and from thence marched to the field of operations. The wily savages refused to give battle, divided their forces into marauding bands, and scattered over the country. The volunteers became discouraged with the dull and futile toil of marching here and there in pursuit of the swift-footed redskins, and when the Indians, finding retreat across the river necessary to avoid battle, left the soil of Illinois, the volunteers refused to follow, and disbanded. The Governor at once called for volunteers from the disorganizing troops, and again Abe stepped forward. But before these new organizations could be perfected and brought into the field, Black Hawk and nearly all his warriors were defeated and captured at the battle of Bad Ax, on the Wisconsin River.

The "veterans" of the Black Hawk war returned home a few days before the fall elections in 1832, and immediately placed their captain in nomination for the Legislature. Abe was little known, except in Salem and the immediate vicinity, and the short time intervening between their return and the election-day prevented any efforts at canvassing the county, but in Salem he beat his opponent nearly two to one.

Soon after, a man named Redford, who had a store in Salem, sold out to a Mr. William G. Greene, who was well acquainted with young Lincoln. Greene proposed to Lincoln and another young man named Berry to take the store off his hands. The copartnership was formed; and Greene became their security to Redford. But Berry proved to be dissolute and dishonest, and the firm of Lincoln and Berry became bankrupt. Lincoln assumed the debt, and set to work to pay it out of his earnings, and at the end of six years had paid the last cent, principal and interest.

During the fall following, while Abe was employed in gathering corn, chopping and hauling wood for the winter, and similar labors, he received the appointment of postmaster from President Jackson. Postage was then high, mails few, and came but twice a week, correspondence meager, and the profits of such a position very small. He could not remain in an office, and so carried the letters *in his hat!* It was somewhat comical to go in quest of the perambulating "post-office," and to find it one day in a cornfield, and the next at a shingle-tree in the woods, but so the literary people of Sangamon were

compelled to do. When a letter, by frequent
contact with the dusky pate upon which the
" United States mail " rested, became worn and
greasy, the postmaster posted it off to the dead-
letter office, with the evidences of its age patent
upon its surface. The office was discontinued,
and no one appeared to take charge of the proceeds, until many years afterward, when Lincoln
was engaged in a thriving and successful practice at law. An agent then called on him and
presented the claim. Lincoln read it over with
an embarrassed look; and some friends who sat
by, supposing he had not the money to pay, drew
out their wallets to assist him. He thanked
them, and said he had almost forgotten what he
had done with that money. But going to an
old trunk in a corner of the office, full of old
papers, pleas, and other office rubbish, he dug
down to the bottom, exhumed a lot of silver
coin, tied up in a faded piece of calico, laid it
upon the table, and counted out the exact sum
which the agent's claim demanded—not a cop-
per more nor less did the rag contain. In all
those years of privation, penury, and toil, he had
not used a cent—even for a brief period—of the
money belonging to the Department.

CHAPTER VI.

SURVEYOR AND LAWYER.

IN the winter of 1834, Abraham obtained a book on surveying, which had an introductory chapter on such principles of geometry and trigonometry as were necessary in the art of measuring heights and distances. This gave him a taste for those sciences, and he did not desist from their pursuit till he had mastered Euclid. He afterward remarked, that from that time he was never satisfied with any argument short of the nearest possible approach to mathematical demonstration.

The following spring he was so fortunate as to have the opportunity to turn his mathematical acquirements to good account. John Calhoun, afterward well known—or rather infamously known—during the Kansas-Nebraska contest of 1855-6, as "Lecompton Calhoun," was then surveyor for Sangamon County. The great immigration into that part of the State gave him more business than he could manage. Hearing of young Lincoln's acquirements in his line, he gave him employment. Abe soon became an accurate and reliable surveyor.

Happening at a book auction, at Springfield, he purchased an old copy of Blackstone's Commentaries, and, as was his habit with any book new to him, plunged at once into the devious mazes of English law. A fresh book to him was as a defiant kingdom to Alexander—a new conquest to be undertaken, and achieved without delay. Alternately surveying for bread and clothing, and wherewithal to buy more books, Abe pushed forward in the study of law. His studio was some shady tree in the edge of the woods in summer, and by a lard lamp at some hospitable fireside in the winter. His devotion to his studies rendered him absent-minded; and some of his neighbors, noticing the change that had come over him, reported that he was becoming insane. These fits of abstraction continued to mark him during the remainder of his life. He would sometimes sit down at the family board, eat mechanically, and without noticing conversation addressed to him; but suddenly recalling himself, as from a dream, he would launch out some witty allusion or quotation of poetry, and at once enter upon the topic which came up in the circle, with great humor and vivacity.

In the fall of 1834, two years after his first candidacy for the Legislature, he was again nominated, and this time elected by a majority of two hundred and fifty above that of the others on his ticket. During this campaign he met his opponent at various places in public debate, and acquitted himself as a logical, witty, and effective public speaker. The State of Illinois was then, and so remained for twenty years afterward, overwhelmingly Democratic, the Whig party forming scarcely a respectable opposition. Had Mr. Lincoln sought popular favor and the honors and emoluments of office, without regard to his convictions of right, he could have placed himself at the head of the party in the State, and shared with Mr. Douglas the political triumphs which that leader achieved; but he was convinced that the principles advocated by the minority were just, that the majority were wrong, and he would not sacrifice an iota of what he regarded as truth for political success or pecuniary gain.

The capital of the state was then at Vandalia,

about one hundred miles from Salem, the home of Mr. Lincoln. The Legislature met in December, when the roads were deep and the weather inclement. But he had not the means to pay his way by public conveyance or to purchase a horse; he therefore walked all the way to the capital, and at the close of the term walked back again. As he returned in the spring the weather was severe, and he, being thinly clad, complained of the cold. One of his colleagues, all of whom were upon horseback, in allusion to his big feet, said : " It is no wonder Abe is cold; *there's so much of him on the ground!*" Lincoln laughed as heartily at this broad joke as any of his companions.

During this session of the Legislature, a series of resolutions were passed pledging the legislators, and, so far as their influence could extend, the people of the State, to vile subserviency to slaveholders. Mr. Lincoln and one other independent and honorable man, DANIEL STONE, would not submit to this humiliation, but entered a vigorous protest upon the journal of the House. By that one manly act " Dan Stone " will be remembered as a just and fearless man, even if all other events of his life are forgotten.

At the close of the second session of the Legislature, Major Stewart, of Springfield, offered him a partnership in the practice of law, which flattering proposal he immediately accepted, and, packing up his scanty wardrobe and library, turned his back upon his old home, with its rough toils, but with its many pleasant associations, for a new and broader field of usefulness. In thus leaving the scene of so many hardships and privations, he also left friends who knew him best and trusted him most—friends who had honored him with his first political success. But mingled with his regret were high hopes as he looked forward to the expanding and brightening future.

The young lawyer did not pack an expensive trunk, with stores of glossy linen, patent collars, and fancy toilet fixtures, as a preparation for this journey to Springfield. He would have been well suited to tie up his extra cotton shirt in a handkerchief, and make a straight line for his new home across lots, taking advantage of his lengthy supply of legs to ford the streams, as he often had done before, and did afterward. But he accumulated a burden of wealth, in the shape of law-books, which he could not carry upon his back. He was, therefore, under the necessity of asking a neighbor boy to haul his box to the Sangamon River, but not to await a passing steamer, as there were none, but to take passage in a vessel of his own. He procured a little skiff, and, loading in his worldly goods, applied his tough hands to the oars, and so "paddled his own canoe" to fortune and fame.

This little incident in Lincoln's life has much in it that is picturesque and pleasing. He had passed the primary grade in his school of discipline. The ax and the maul, the scanty clothing and penury, the struggle for education and culture against most discouraging disadvantages, all were left behind as he stepped from the bank of the stream into his little boat. He was now to test his powers in efforts of intellect instead of muscle. He doubtless looked to success in the legal profession as the summit of his ambition, not knowing that this, also, was merely a higher school of discipline to prepare him for the work of his life.

His success at the law was immediate. Political campaigning had given him fluency and confidence as a public speaker; and his acute and logical mind was peculiarly fitted for the work of that controversial profession. The next Legislative election the people of Springfield returned him for a second term to the Legislature; this was repeated from time to time, till his professional duties became so onerous that he was compelled to decline further service in that body.

CHAPTER VII.

HIS COURSE AS A LAWYER.

RICKERY and deception are regarded as vices almost inseparable from the legal profession. In almost every contest one or both of the parties are seeking to do injustice. The attorney is constantly brought in contact with knavery, becomes familiar with all its devious ways, and is often strongly tempted, by pecuniary gain and professional ambition, to resort to it himself. And yet the most certain avenue to success in this, as in other callings, is unswerving honesty. No business man is willing to incur the vexation, watchfulness, and, withal, the uncertainty, of dealing with a knave. On the other hand, business intercourse with a man of Christian uprightness and integrity is a constant source of satisfaction and security.

Mr. Lincoln's course as a lawyer was "obstinately honest." So thorough was the confidence

4

reposed in him by those who knew him well,
that with them his logical deductions, in addressing a jury, would outweigh the testimony
upon oath of some respectable witnesses. Constantly acting upon principle, he could not and
would not defend the wrong. He not only would
not lie for any man or any cause, but he would
have nothing to do with a cause for the maintenance of which it was necessary for *any body*
to lie.

During the progress of an important trial at
Springfield, he became convinced that his client
was acting dishonestly, and that justice and the
law were against him. He at once notified his
associate counsel that he would not argue such
a case, and took no further part in it. The trial
proceeded, and, much to Mr. Lincoln's astonish-
ment, his colleague gained the verdict. The
successful client paid over to the firm the hand-
some fee of nine hundred dollars, but Mr. Lincoln would not accept a dime of it.

At that time it was customary, as now, for the
common pleas judges to pass from county to
county, holding courts in each, with the difference that the judicial districts embraced a much
wider area of country than at present. It was

also the custom of the best lawyers to follow the judges from one county to another, and thus extend their practice over the whole district. This was called "circuit riding," a term applied to the itinerant labors of both lawyers and preachers.

The minister and the lawyer, each equipped with saddle-bags and leggings, pursued their journeys on horseback, through mud and rain, snow and sleet, through sloughs and across rivers, contented and happy in the pursuit of their callings.

While engaged in studying his profession in intervals of hard labor, in Menard County, a family named Armstrong, father, mother, and sons, had kindly made him welcome to a home in their cabin during one winter. This generous hospitality from a poor man, as Armstrong then was, was treasured in the grateful memory of the rising lawyer, and brought a full reward, as the following incident, related by one who witnessed it, fully shows:

"Some few years since, the oldest son of Mr. Lincoln's old friend Armstrong, the chief support of his widowed mother—the good old man having some time previously passed from earth—

was arrested on the charge of murder. A young man had been killed during a riotous mêlée in the night-time, at a camp-meeting, and one of his associates stated that the death-wound was inflicted by young Armstrong. A preliminary examination was gone into, at which the accuser testified so positively that there seemed to be no doubt of the guilt of the prisoner, and, therefore, he was held for trial. As is too often the case, the bloody act caused an undue excitement in the public mind. Every improper incident in the life of the prisoner, each act which bore the least resemblance to rowdyism, each school-boy quarrel, was suddenly remembered and magnified, until they pictured him as a fiend of the most horrid hue. As these rumors were spread abroad they were received as gospel truth, and the most feverish desire for vengeance seized upon the infatuated populace, while only prison-bars prevented a horrible death at the hands of a mob. The events were heralded in the newspapers, painted in the highest colors, accompanied with rejoicing over the certainty of punishment being meted out to the guilty party. The prisoner, overwhelmed by the circumstances in which he found himself placed, fell into a melancholy condition bordering on despair; and the widowed mother, looking through her tears, saw no cause for hope from earthly aid.

" At this juncture the widow received a letter from Mr. Lincoln, volunteering his services in an effort to save the youth from the impending stroke. Gladly was his aid accepted, although it seemed impossible for even his sagacity to prevail in such a desperate case; but the heart of the attorney was in the work, and he set about it with a will that knew no such word as fail. Feeling that the poisoned condition of the public mind was such as to preclude the possibility of impaneling an impartial jury in the court having jurisdiction, he procured a change of venue and a postponement of the trial. He then went studiously to work unraveling the history of the case, and satisfied himself that his client was the victim of malice, and that the statements of the accuser were a tissue of falsehoods. When the trial was called, the prisoner, pale and emaciated, and with hopelessness written on every feature—accompanied by his half-hoping, half-despairing mother, whose only hope was a mother's belief in her son's innocence, in the justice of God, and in the noble counsel who, without hope of fee or reward on earth, had undertaken the cause—took his seat in the prisoner's box, and with stony firmness listened to the reading of the indictment.

"Lincoln sat quietly by, while the large auditory looked on him as though wondering what he could say in defense of one whose guilt was deemed certain. The examination of the witnesses for the State was begun, and a well-arranged mass of evidence, circumstantial and positive, was introduced, which seemed to impale the prisoner beyond the possibility of extrication. Mr. Lincoln propounded but few questions, and those of a character which excited no uneasiness on the part of the prosecutor, merely, in most cases, requiring the main witness to be definite as to time and place. When the evidence of the prosecution was closed, Lincoln introduced a few witnesses to remove some erroneous impressions in regard to the previous character of his client, who, though somewhat rowdyish, had never been known to commit a vicious act, and to show that a greater degree of ill-feeling existed between the accuser and the accused than between the accused and the murdered man. The prosecutor felt that the case was a clear one, and his opening speech was brief and formal.

"Lincoln arose, while a deathly silence pervaded the vast audience, and, in a clear but moderate tone, began his argument. Slowly and carefully he reviewed the testimony, pointing out the hitherto unobserved discrepancies in the statements of the principal witness. That which appeared plain and plausible he made to appear crooked as a serpent's path. The witness had stated that the affair took place at a certain hour in the evening, and that, by the aid of the brightly-shining moon, he saw the prisoner inflict the death-blow with a slung-shot. Mr. Lincoln showed that at the hour referred to the moon was not yet above the horizon, and, consequently, the whole tale was a fabrication. He then drew a picture of the perjurer so horrid and ghastly that the accuser could sit under it no longer, but reeled and staggered from the court-room. Then, in words of thrilling pathos, Lincoln appealed to the jurors as fathers of sons who might become fatherless, to yield to no previous impressions of ill-founded prejudice, but to do his client justice; and as he alluded to the debt of gratitude which he owed the boy's sire, tears

were seen to fall from many eyes unused to
weep. It was near night, when he concluded by
saying that if justice were done, as he believed
it would be, before the sun should set it would
shine upon his client a free man. Half an hour
had not elapsed when a messenger announced
that the jury had agreed upon their verdict.
The court-room was soon filled to overflowing
by citizens of the town. When the prisoner and
his mother entered, silence reigned as completely
as if the house were empty. The foreman of the
jury, in answer to the usual inquiry from the
court, in a strong, clear tone, announced the
verdict, "NOT GUILTY!" The widow dropped
into the arms of her son, who held her up, and
told her to look on him as before, a free man
and innocent. Then, with the words, "Where
is Mr. Lincoln?" he rushed across the room and
grasped the hand of his deliverer, while his
heart was too full for utterance. Lincoln turned
his eyes toward the west, where the sun still
lingered in view, and then turning toward the
youth, said, "It is not yet sundown, and you
are free."

While riding alone, at one time, to attend court
in a neighboring county, an incident occurred

which would have seemed strange and ludicrous
to a bystander, and which yet gives a view of
the humane and sensitive heart of Mr. Lincoln,
and shows that, in the quality of mercy, he was
as child-like and sincere as he was determined
in his ideas of truth and justice.

He was riding by a deep slough, in which
he saw a pig ingulfed, and showing by its exhausted efforts that it would never succeed in
extricating itself. He looked at it a moment
with a pitying eye, but the mud was deep and
black, and his wardrobe for the journey was
limited to the suit he had on. He therefore
rode on, but more than once looked back at the
pitiable object. Pursuing his way about two
miles, during which time he sought in vain to
banish the struggling pig from his mind, he
turned suddenly about and rode quickly back,
fearing he might be too late to save the animal's
life. Dismounting, he hitched his horse and set
about his labor of mercy in good earnest. He
soon had a bridge of rails built to within
reach of the pig, seized him by the ears and
landed him on *terra firma*. After looking at him
with a smile, as he scampered off, he re-mounted
his horse and rode away. Mr. Lincoln probably

never in his life inflicted wanton pain on the sensibilities of any person, or upon the humblest of God's creatures. But while

> " Meekly bending heart and brow
> To the helpless and the low "—

was also ever

> " Ready to redress the wrong
> Of the weak against the strong."

After he had attained power and fame, his former humble and illiterate friends found him the same unassuming, considerate, and affectionate friend that he was while sharing their hospitality as a poor boy at the cabin fireside, or around the homely meal. Having one night left his comfortable quarters and agreeable companions, at the hotel of a village where he was attending court, to visit an aged friend in her cabin, his friends remonstrated with him. " O," said he, " it would break old Aunty's heart to hear that I had left town without visiting her." He took pleasure, and it was pleasure in its highest and noblest form, in seating himself at the old matron's table, to listen to her garrulous talk, relate his merriest stories, and gratify her by his unaffected respect.

An incident in wide contrast to these, and which brought out wholly different traits of his character, took place in 1839. The Legislature was then in session at Springfield, and Mr. Lincoln was a member. During the session, a young lady wrote, and the editor of the paper at Springfield published, a sarcastic poem, which the public at once understood as directed against James Shields, also a member of the Legislature. Shields demanded of the editor the name of so audacious a writer, with the intent to repay the shedding of ink by the shedding of blood. Lincoln was unmarried, and understood to be at least an admirer of the offending young lady, and the editor, dishonorably fearing to meet the responsibility, repaired to Lincoln, with the request that he would assume it, and settle the difficulty with Shields. He at once consented, and Shields was informed that Lincoln considered himself responsible.

Mr. Lincoln seems to have gone into this difficulty without thinking of its folly—his mind absorbed with the idea of defending the name and privacy of the lady. Shields immediately challenged him to mortal combat, and Lincoln as promptly accepted, naming broad-swords as the weapons, and " Bloody Island " in the Illinois river as the place. At the time appointed, Shields and his friends, and a surgeon, repaired to the place, and found Abe busy chopping away the underbrush with his sword, to clear a place for the duel. Friends who knew the trivial nature of the quarrel interfered and put an end to it. Lincoln said, doubtless truly, that he did not intend to injure Shields, and chose broad-swords that his superior reach of arm might enable him to defend himself and disarm his antagonist; but even with this purpose, it was the most unreasonable act of his life.

CHAPTER VIII.

MARRIAGE.

IN 1842 Mr. Lincoln was thirty-three years old, and established in a flourishing practice at law. He therefore deemed himself of sufficient age, and in possession of resources adequate, for the maintenance of a family. Accordingly he sought and won the heart and hand of Miss Mary Todd, daughter of Hon. Robert S. Todd, of Lexington, Ky. His bride had resided in Springfield for several years previous to her marriage, and doubtless fully appreciated the value of the " rough diamond " she had chosen. His social nature and kind disposition fitted him to enjoy the attractions of a home, and his wit, drollery, and genuine hospitality to render it singularly attractive to inmates and friends. His private correspondence at this time shows how happy he was in his new relation, and in the new cares and motives for exertion which that relation brought upon him.

One afternoon, while sitting in the law-office with his partner, Wm. Herndon, Esq., busily employed in his professional labors, a poverty-stricken old negro woman, with care and sorrow depicted on her furrowed face, came in and requested an interview. She and her children had been slaves in Kentucky, and their master had brought them into Illinois and set them free. Her son obtained employment as steward on a river steamer plying between Springfield and New Orleans, and supported her by his wages. Imprudently stepping off the boat at the latter city, he was seized by the rapacious police, under the assumed authority of the laws of Louisiana against the immigration of free negroes, and hurried off to prison, where he was liable to be sold into perpetual slavery in payment of his fine. Mr. Lincoln heard the story, and requested Mr. Herndon to go to Gov. Bissell, whose office was near at hand, and request his interference. Bissell replied that the Constitution gave him no right whatever to call in question the laws of a Southern State. On hearing this, Lincoln sprang to his feet in great excitement, struck his desk with clinched hand, and exclaimed, "I'll have that negro back, or I'll have such an agitation in Illinois that the Governor will *learn* his constitutional rights!" It did not become necessary for Mr. Lincoln to make his threatened appeal for justice to the people. The colored man was recovered by the New Orleans authorities and restored to his aged mother.

Not unfrequently fugitive slaves were pursued, in their eager flight for freedom, and captured in Mr. Lincoln's district, or in the vicinity. But such was the terror which the epithet "Abolitionist" or "nigger thief" inspired that most lawyers were unwilling to incur the odium of defending them before the courts. But Lincoln in Illinois, like Chase in Ohio, and Stephens in Pennsylvania, never quailed before that cruel, black, and bloody power. He stood between it and its trembling victims, defending them to the utmost, whenever called upon. Other lawyers said, "It is right and just to defend these fugitives, but we have political aspirations, and can not afford it." Lincoln and Chase had aspirations too, but they could not afford to unman and degrade themselves. The one became President and the other Chief Justice of the

United States, by regarding *justice* as the first
object to be sought; while of all that herd of
pliant politicians, scarce one is known beyond
a limited circle.

In 1846 Mr. Lincoln sought and obtained a
nomination for Congress in the Sangamon district, and after a spirited canvass was elected
by a majority of 1,511 votes—597 greater than
the same district had given the year before to
that polished and popular statesman Henry Clay,
as candidate for the Presidency. The great
lights of the past generation were then in the
legislative halls—Clay, Webster, Calhoun, Ben-
ton, and Adams. Those men, though probably
not superior in intellect and eloquence to many
now occupying their places, exerted a wider influence and control than men of equal powers
could do now. That was the era in our country's history for the leadership of *men*. The
mighty struggle of a later day reversed this order, and gave the country the leadership of the
masses. The personal fortunes of the leader
were then an object of interest; they are now
wholly disregarded. The people use the men
who seem best adapted to serve their purposes;
the moment he proves himself unfit, unwilling,

or inadequate, he is cast aside with as little regret as the artisan casts aside a worthless instrument, which is a change greatly for the
better. Mr. Lincoln made a respectable legislator, but did not succeed in rising above the
shadow cast by those great names.

At the close of his Congressional term, in
1849, Mr. Lincoln returned to the quiet routine
of his profession, taking little part in politics,
but by no means indifferent to the questions of
importance in the political world, as they arose.
His next appearance in public life was in a controversy far more grand in its proportions and
glorious in its results than any that had taxed
the strength of true patriots since the close of
the American Revolution. The better to understand the circumstances of this contest, let us
briefly recur to the aggressive power by whom
it was forced upon the country, and for the
struggle with which God had trained Abraham
Lincoln from his mother's knee.

5

CHAPTER IX.

THE IRREPRESSIBLE CONFLICT.

FRICAN slavery and the slave-trade were first introduced into Morocco, Spain, and Portugal, by the Moors, nearly seven hundred years ago. After the banishment of that race from their possessions in Europe, the Spaniards and Portuguese seized upon the abhorrent traffic, and have practiced it continually since, even after other nations had pronounced it piracy and punished it with death. From that cruel and unprincipled people the New World received that spirit of oppression and sham-chivalry which became such a mighty power for wickedness in our hemisphere. The tortures inflicted by Pizarro in Peru, by Cortez in Mexico, and by the rebels at Andersonville, are all parts of the same cast, actuated by the same spirit, and repeating age after age, the same bombastic ideas, stilted forms of expression, and the same cruel practices.

The slave-trade was introduced in the Western Hemisphere by Christopher Columbus, on his first voyage. He beguiled a number of unsuspecting natives on board of his ship, the Santa Maria, when on the point of starting on his return, took them to Spain, and sold them into slavery. They were, however, afterward liberated, by order of Queen Isabella. The colonists, who followed in the wake of Columbus, also followed his example; but the aboriginal tribes withered and perished under the hard hand of the implacable Spanish task-master. At the professedly pious suggestion of Las Casas, a Jesuit missionary, the Spaniards sent vessels direct to the coast of Guinea, to capture the hardier Africans and import them to supply the demand. The system, once introduced, spread rapidly in every colony planted in the New World—Portuguese, Dutch, English, and French.

Ten years after the first cargo of slaves was landed in St. Augustine, Florida, the Mayflower, freighted with Puritans and free principles, touched the Plymouth Rock. From that day began the growth of two hostile systems on American soil—incongruous and antagonistic as fire and water—each intolerant of the life of the other. The conflict began and continued with increasing violence till the death-blow was dealt by Abraham Lincoln; and that its doom might be irrevocably sealed, Providence permitted the vanquished system to close its infamous history with a crime that filled mankind with horror.

True, the lines between the conflicting moral forces were not, in point of geographical location, distinctly drawn. Georgia, at an early day, and before she became a colony of the British crown, prohibited slavery and rum; while New England both manufactured the one and practiced the other. But the principles of the Puritans gathered clearness and strength in the rugged hills of the North, while the dark spirit of slavery spread and intensified its hideous reign along the malarious levels of the southern coast.

When the war of the Revolution was terminated by the triumph of the colonies, and the statesmen of that day assembled at Philadelphia, in 1787, to frame a government for our then independent country, the population consisted of a little less than three millions, of whom one-sixth, or near five hundred thousand, were African slaves. That convention was almost unanimously opposed to the continued existence of the system of bondage, but they unwisely and unrighteously yielded to the determined spirit of caste and oppression, and inaugurated those wicked compromises with the evil, which have borne such bitter fruits of sorrow and blood.

From this time forward slavery grew in extent, in wealth and influence, as it also did in the intensity and malignance of its cruel spirit. Every department in the organization of society was invaded and held. The church was corrupted, the press subsidized, the highest seats of justice occupied, the new territories, as far as possible, overrun and secured, popular education suppressed, the freedom of speech and of the press abridged, the minds of the people poisoned with disloyalty and treason, and finally the boundaries and authority of the system declared to be coëxtensive and coëqual with those of the free Republic.

In pursuance of this arrogant pretension, an attempt was made to seize upon the territories of Kansas and Nebraska, which had been solemnly pledged to freedom, and a decision of the Supreme Court obtained at the hand of Chief Justice Taney, whose memory, by that act, is now buried in infamy, known as the Dred Scott decision, which rendered the free States themselves slave territory.

These tremendous strides of usurpation alarmed the people of the free States, and in 1854 they combined, under the name of the Republican party, to resist its further encroachments.

Stephen A. Douglas, a Senator from Illinois, a man of great intellectual power combined with political sagacity, though but little influenced by moral principle, had become the leader and champion of the slave power. He led in the contest which resulted in the violation of the compact between the free and slave States, known as the Missouri Compromise, and had much to do in concocting and sustaining the decision of Judge Taney, before alluded to. At the organization of the Republican party, Mr. Lincoln at once entered into the spirit of that combination, with his whole soul and energy. During the years of his seclusion from political life, he had grown steadily in intellectual strength and resource. His wise, original, and practical methods of thought had received rhetorical polish, and his delivery, though not that of the finished orator, had acquired vivacity and force. When, therefore, Mr. Douglas, the "Little Giant,"

as his admirers delighted to style him, returned
to his constituency to ask their approval of his
policy, the friends of freedom put Mr. Lincoln
forth, as the ablest man in their ranks, to grap-
ple with this champion of the slave power. He
accepted the task with alacrity. To deal un-
sparing blows upon oppression, injustice, and
cruelty, and to advocate the principles involved
in the Golden Rule, was a work which aroused
all the enthusiasm of his nature, and armed
anew every power of his mind. He had for his
antagonist one esteemed among the first intellects
of the nation, strengthened by long experience,
untiring industry, and by unscrupulous cunning,
and animated by unconquerable ambition.

The great contestants were not long in coming in collision. In October, 1864, the State
Fair for Illinois was held at Springfield, and Mr.
Douglas improved the opportunity to deliver a
carefully-prepared and elaborate defense of his
course. He affirmed that the people of each territory should determine for themselves whether
they should form a free or a slaveholding State.
This enunciation he styled the " great principle
of popular sovereignty." He maintained that
this Government was instituted solely for the

benefit of white people; that the declaration in the Declaration of Independence that "all men are born free and equal" only meant that British subjects in the colonies were equal in their rights with British subjects in England; that the decision in the Dred Scott case was the supreme law, and as such must be respected and obeyed by all good citizens; and denounced the Republicans as being favorable to the admixture of the white and black races.

Mr. Lincoln replied the following day. The Springfield Journal thus pictures the scene: "He quivered with feeling and emotion. The whole house was still as death. He attacked the Senator's Kansas-Nebraska Bill with warmth and energy, and all felt that a man of strength was its enemy, and that he intended to blast it, if he could, by his strong and manly efforts. He was most successful, and the house approved the glorious triumph of truth by loud and long-continued huzzas. He exhibited the bill in all its aspects, to show its humbuggery and falsehood; and when thus torn to tatters and held up to the vast crowd, a kind of scorn was visible upon the face of the crowd and upon the lips of the eloquent speaker. At the conclusion of the speech, every man felt that it was unanswerable; that no human power could overthrow it or trample it under foot."

As a specimen passage from this argument, the following may be quoted: "My distinguished friend says it is an insult to the emigrants to Kansas and Nebraska to suppose that they are not able to govern themselves. We must not slur over an argument of this kind because it happens to tickle the ear. It must be met and answered. I admit that the emigrant to Kansas and Nebraska is competent to govern himself, but (the speaker rising to his full height) I DENY HIS RIGHT TO GOVERN ANY OTHER PERSON WITHOUT THAT PERSON'S CONSENT." Never was a sophistry more hopelessly impaled than was Mr. Douglas's "great principle" by that one sharp and luminous sentence.

The next discussion was held, a few days after, at Peoria. Mr. Lincoln's triumph here was even more signal than at Springfield. One of his happy rejoinders was as follows: "In the course of my main argument, Judge Douglas interrupted me to say that the principle of the Nebraska Bill was very old; that it originated when God made man, and placed good and evil before him, allowing him to choose for himself, being responsible for the choice he should make. At the time I thought that this was merely playful, and I answered it accordingly; but in his reply to me he renewed it as a serious argument. In seriousness, then, the facts of his proposition are not true, as stated. God did not place good and evil before man, telling him to make his choice. On the contrary, he did tell him there was one tree of the fruit of which, if he ate, *he should surely die.* I could scarcely wish so strong a prohibition of slavery in Nebraska."

In 1858 occurred the most memorable political canvass, at a State election, that the country has ever witnessed. Mr. Douglas's term of office as United States Senator was about to expire, and it would devolve upon the Legislature of the State to be chosen at that election to appoint his successor. The Democratic Convention which assembled to nominate State officers also named Mr. Douglas as their choice for Senator, and the Republicans, following their example, nominated Abraham Lincoln. Douglas received, soon after, a challenge from Lincoln to canvass the State in friendly public discussions. They accordingly met and debated the questions at

issue before immense audiences in various parts
of the State.   The manner in which Mr. Lincoln acquitted himself in these debates may be
judged by the fact that they were collected and
published in full, giving Mr. Douglas's speeches
without abridgment, by the Republicans in other
States, and circulated free as campaign docu-
ments.

The result of this campaign was that the Republicans carried the State by about five thousand majority, but a large number of Democratic
legislators who had been elected the previous
year held their offices at the next session, and
were sufficient to overcome Mr. Lincoln's gain
and reëlect Mr. Douglas.   But such was the
enthusiasm aroused for the defeated aspirant,
that he was immediately named ir various parts
of the North as the Republican candidate for
the Presidency in 1860—rather a remarkable
result for a defeated politician.

Mr. Douglas was as able a political debater
as our country has produced.   He had not the
breadth and stateliness of Webster, nor the finish
and brilliance of Clay, but in readiness, audacity,
compression of style, and in dauntless courage
he had no superior.   He lacked nothing to place

him among the first of American orators and statesmen, except that high moral principle which prefers truth and right to every inferior consideration. He accomplished much for the material prosperity of his State, and for the temporary triumphs of his party. He exhibited on many occasions the elements of profound statesmanship and far-reaching forecast; and had the American people been dealing with questions of material interest merely, his reputation would be different from what it now is. But the issues contested before the people directly involved the laws of God concerning the rights of man. With all his sagacity and knowledge he did not know that those laws are far mightier than the ablest inventions of man, and that they would vindicate themselves to the defeat and shame of any man or party who undertook to trample them beneath their feet. Mr. Lincoln did most thoroughly understand this great truth. He sought footing on those resistless moral forces, God's laws, and by them, not by his own intellectual powers, was carried forward over prostrate opposition to enduring triumph. On the contrary, Mr. Douglas, with all his rare intellectual gifts, his wide influence, his oft-repeated political victories, his life has gone into history as one of disappointment and failure—failure which he deeply and bitterly felt during the last few months of his life.

The history of the past is strewn with such wrecks. Every generation presents examples to prove beyond cavil the fact that HONESTY, TRUTH, JUSTICE, and the other virtues enjoined by the Savior, are absolutely essential to a life that can, in any true sense, be either successful or happy.

CHAPTER X.

THE PRESIDENTIAL CONTEST.

IN the spring of 1860, Mr. Lincoln received pressing invitations to visit and address the people in New York and New England. He accepted the call, and was heartily welcomed in several Eastern cities. In Cooper Institute, **New York city**, he delivered his last and perhaps **most brilliant** political address as a citizen, and one which, perhaps more than any other event, fixed the hearts of the people upon him as their choice for the next President.

During his stay in that city, he started out one Sabbath morning alone, and wandered into a mission Sabbath-school. The teacher, in describing the incident, says : " Our Sunday-school in the Five Points was assembled one Sabbath morning, a few months since, when I noticed a tall and remarkable-looking man enter the room and take a seat among us. He listened with fixed attention to our exércises, and his countenance manifested such genuine interest that I approached him, and suggested that he might be willing to say something to the children. He accepted the invitation with evident pleasure, and, coming forward, began a simple address, which at once fascinated every little hearer and hushed the room to silence. His language was strikingly beautiful, ███████ es musical, with intensest feel███ around would droop into s█ █████ ered sentences of warning, █████ nto sunshine as he spoke chee███ ████ romise. Once or twice he attempted to close his remarks, but the imperative shout, 'Go on!' 'O, do go on!' would compel him to resume. As I looked upon the gaunt and sinewy frame of the stranger, and marked his powerful head and determined features, now touched into softness by the impressions of the moment, I felt an irrepressible curiosity to know something more about him, and as he was quietly leaving the room, I begged to know his name. He courteously replied, ' It is Abraham Lincoln, from Illinois.' "

On the 16th day of May the Republican Na-

tional Convention met at Chicago, Illinois. The
two most prominent candidates were William H.
Seward, of New York, and Mr. Lincoln, and
great efforts were made by the friends of each
to secure the nomination of their candidate.
Mr. Seward had thus far in his life been an
able, tolerably consistent, and very eloquent
friend of freedom. He was recognized as the
most accomplished and capable statesman in the
Republican ran███████████████therefore,
numerous and███████████████On the
first ballot he███████████████er of
votes that wer███████████████not a
majority of all t███████████████the second
ballot, those who h███████████████their ballots
for Mr. Chase, Mr. W██de, and others, combined
upon Mr. Lincoln, and he was nominated for
the Presidency. The result was hailed throughout the whole North with the wildest demon-
strations of joy. In November he was elected
by great majorities in every Northern State, his
vote in the electoral college being 180 to 123.

The slaveholding States had not only antici-
pated this result, but did indirectly what they
could to secure it, intending to make it a pretext for rebellion. No sooner was the result

ABRAHAM LINCOLN LEAVING ILLINOIS.

announced than the slave States at once began the most vigorous preparations for war. ✦In December South Carolina seceded, and seized upon Fort Moultrie, in Charleston harbor. During January the other States lying upon the Gulf (except Texas, which followed the first day of the next month), seceded, and seized upon the forts and arsenals within their limits; and on the 9th of February the rebel government was organized at Montgomery, Alabama, by the election of Jefferson Davis as President. War was inevitable, and the weak and corrupt old politician James Buchanan, then President, permitted every influence of his high office to be used by his traitorous officials in strengthening the rebel cause and in preparing to overthrow the Government.

Mr. Lincoln foresaw the tremendous ordeal through which he was called to pass as the President of the nation, but calmly awaited, at his home in Springfield, till the time should come when his work was to begin. He had foreseen it clearly before his election, and relied upon the almighty arm of God with implicit confidence, and with the humble dependence of a little child. In a most serious conversation with a friend, a few days before the election took place, he alluded to the fact that many prominent ministers of the Gospel and professing Christians of his own town intended to vote for the pro-slavery candidates. "I have carefully read the Bible, and I do not so understand this book," he said, as he drew from his bosom a pocket Testament. "These men well know that I am for freedom in the territories, for freedom every-where, as far as the Constitution and laws will permit, and that my opponents are for slavery. They *know* this, and yet, with this book in their hands, in the light of which human bondage can not live for a moment, they are going to vote against me. I do not understand it at all." With cheeks wet with tears, and a trembling voice, he continued: "I know there is a God, and that he hates slavery and injustice. I see the storm coming, and I know that his hand is in it. If he has a place and work for me, and I believe he has, I believe I am ready. I am nothing, but truth and justice are every thing. I know that I am right, because I know that liberty is right; for Christ teaches it, and Christ is God. I have told them that a house divided against itself can not stand, and Christ and reason say the same, and they will find it so. Douglas does not care whether slavery is voted up or down, but God cares, and humanity cares, and I care; and with God's help I shall not fail. I may not see the end, but it will come, and I shall be vindicated; and these men will find that they have not read their Bibles aright." Pausing a moment, and walking to and fro across the room in silence, he resumed: "A revelation could not make it plainer to me than that slavery or the Government must be destroyed. The future would be something awful to me but for this rock upon which I stand [holding up the Testament in his hand]. It seems to me that God has borne with this thing [slavery] until the very teachers of religion claim for it a divine sanction and character; and now the cup of iniquity is full and the vials will be poured out."

In alluding to his secret feeling to this friend, he said: "I think more on these subjects [the providence, protection, and justice of God] than upon all others, and have done so for years." These years of thoughtful contemplation of the justice, faithfulness, and sovereignty of God were not an hour longer than was needed to establish his mind and prepare him to look calmly and fearlessly into the black future that lay before him. One ray only lit up the gloomy prospect, but that was the light of God. Lincoln fixed his eyes upon it and stepped forward, "without fear and with a manly heart." *

The hoarse roar of treason, falsehood, and rage arose from the Atlantic to the Mississippi; such, in fact, as we may imagine arises from that congregation of evil ones to which God forever banishes his implacable enemies and the enemies of mankind. The nations awaited with absorbing interest the impending burst of the tempest. In the midst of it he prepared for his departure for Washington, and on the 11th of February bade good-bye to his home and friends, whom he was never again to visit while living. Addressing them, he said: " My friends, no one not in my position can appreciate the sadness I

---

* The question whether Mr. Lincoln was truly a converted man at this time has given rise to difference of opinion. His intellectual belief in our Lord Jesus Christ was clear and strong, and his confidence *may* have been based upon logical conclusions concerning God's attributes and providence, without any experimental knowledge of his saving love. This interesting subject will be more fully discussed in a succeeding chapter.

feel at this parting. To this people I owe all that I am. Here have I lived for more than a quarter of a century. Here my children were born, and here one of them lies buried. I know not how soon I shall see you again. A duty devolves upon me which is greater, perhaps, than that which has devolved upon any other man since the days of Washington. He never would have succeeded except for the aid of Divine Providence, upon which he at all times relied. I feel that I can not succeed without the same divine aid which sustained him, and on the same almighty Being I place my reliance for support; and I hope you, my friends, will pray that I may receive that divine assistance without which I can not succeed, but with which success is certain. Again I bid you an affectionate farewell."

As he progressed in his journey he was received with the grandest displays of affection and honor by a nation who felt that, under God, their lives, and liberties, and national existence were in his hands.

Intense anxiety pervaded the nation to discover the feelings and plans of the new President. He was called upon at almost every

station for a speech; and as he could not
prudently divulge any plans he may have enter-
tained, or use expressions which might be con-
strued to inflame to a greater degree the malig-
nant passions of the rising rebels, or otherwise
complicate the difficulty, his brief addresses were
necessarily tame and unsatisfactory, and calculated to fill the hearts of patriots with anxious
forebodings.

At Philadelphia, as he was about to leave the
loyal States and take his journey through a
part of the country where slavery prevailed, he
learned of the discovery of a conspiracy at Baltimore to assassinate him. Taking a train the
evening before the day on which he was expected
in that city, he passed through in safety.

The aged hero and patriot WINFIELD SCOTT,
then Commander-in-chief of the United States
Army, was in Washington during the inauspi-
cious months between Mr. Lincoln's election
and his inauguration. He did all he could to
induce the weak and traitorous President, James
Buchanan, to prepare the country for the impending storm of war, but without avail. On
learning the approach of Mr. Lincoln, he gathered the few soldiers stationed at Washington,

and organized them for the protection of the Government, and arranged with such patriotic citizens as were to be found in the city for volunteer reënforcements, should the emergency require them. Mr. Lincoln, on his arrival, was conducted to a public hotel, and the following day the usual ceremonies of the inauguration proceeded without disturbance. Chief Justice Taney, though very old, still discharged the duties of his high office, and administered the oath to Mr. Lincoln. As he thus legalized the stamp of condemnation which the people had placed upon his wicked decision, his reflections must have been gloomy. He could not but foresee that his name would go down to posterity inseparably associated with the infamous attempt he had made to destroy justice and establish oppression upon the prostrate rights of man.

The inaugural was delivered in a clear and distinct tone, touched, at times, with pathos and softened with expostulation. In it the new President exhausted all his powers of reason and persuasion, in an effort to disabuse the minds of the rebels, and bring them peaceably back to their allegiance. His absorbing desire to avert the horrors of war overshadowed every other

thought, and he plead with those determined traitors as a father would plead with his wayward
sons. He concluded by saying : " In your
hands, my dissatisfied fellow-countrymen, and
not in mine, is the momentous issue of civil war.
The Government will not assail you. You can
have no conflict without being yourselves the
aggressors. You can have no oath registered
in heaven to destroy the Government, while I
have the most solemn one to ' preserve, protect,
and defend ' it.

" I am loth to close. We are not enemies,
but friends. We must not be enemies. Though
passion may have strained, it must not break
the bonds of affection. The mystic cords of
memory, stretching from every patriot grave
and battle-field to every living heart and hearth-
stone all over this broad land, will yet swell the
chorus of the Union when touched again, as
they surely will be, by the better angels of our
nature."

These solemn and touching words were received by the rebels and their friends in Baltimore, Cincinnati, Richmond, Charleston, and
elsewhere, with outcries of vituperation and con-
temptuous sneers. God had " prepared to pour

out his vials of wrath." The tongue of an angel could not have softened those traitor hearts.

Mr. Lincoln proceeded to organize his cabinet and prepare for the trying emergencies which obviously hastened upon him, trusting, however, that some peaceable exit might be found from the difficulties which beset the Government. Meantime the fully-organized " Confederacy " at Montgomery used every exertion to concentrate and strengthen their cause, and to make their first intended blow fatal to the Government. Their newspapers and orators were full of boasting and intimidation. They sang the triumphant songs of victory before the battle began, and gloated in imagination over the prostrate land of liberty :

"In dreams through camp and court they bore
The trophies of the conqueror."

Abraham Lincoln and the loyal Christian people of the land labored and prayed as Americans never labored and prayed before. On the 17th of April the storm burst on Sumter, enveloping that fortress in a shower of bombs and wrapping it in consuming fire.

We have now arrived at a period in the life

of Abraham Lincoln where the grandest events crowded thick and fast upon him and upon the country. To write his life as it transpired during the succeeding four years, would be to write the history of the greatest civil war ever waged upon the globe. And were such a task within the capacity of this volume, or of the writer, it would be wholly beyond the object sought in this biography. Let us trace only such incidents as more directly illustrate his character and the principles by which he was actuated.

CHAPTER XI.

THE CALL TO ARMS.

THE news of the bombardment of Sumter flew on the wings of the lightning to every hamlet and home in our broad Union, and instantly patriotic millions sprang to their feet, looking eagerly to Mr. Lincoln, and ready for his word of command. He hastily drew up his proclamation for seventy-five thousand men, a number which, in the light of later events, appears strangely inadequate to the task before them. Mr. Douglas, the life-long political antagonist of Mr. Lincoln, and the champion of this very power now in arms, could not resist the appeal. On the evening before it was issued, he visited Mr. Lincoln at his private apartments, listened to the proclamation, and gave it his hearty approval, except in the number of men called to arms, which he recommended should be made at least two hundred thousand. The two former rivals and contestants sat in earnest consultation, Mr. Lincoln listening with gratified and eager interest to the advice which Mr. Douglas, from his intimate acquaintance with the leaders in his great conspiracy prepared him well to give. They parted, and with the President's call, the next morning, went the cheering intelligence that Lincoln and Douglas were standing side by side and shoulder to shoulder in the support of the Government. This was almost the last, and was the most honorable act, of Mr. Douglas's life. Within a few weeks he returned on a visit to his home in Illinois, where he became sick and died.

With the answering thousands to Mr. Lincoln's proclamation came cares and duties to his office more arduous and wearing than had ever crowded upon any former Chief Magistrate. Where hundreds were expected, thousands flew to the rescue of the imperiled Government. These raw volunteers had to be armed, clothed, organized, and led. The civil officers, to a great extent, were filled with traitors; these had to be removed and true men appointed. The vast army rising quickly, almost as a vision, must be

officered; and for the vacancies in these two
departments came thousands of applicants, who
beset Mr. Lincoln by night and by day, and he
gave audience and a word to all who could crowd
into his presence. The rebels were powerful in
numbers, and led by men of surpassing ability.
The Democratic party of the North was suspi-
cious of their late political antagonists, and had
to be managed with caution and profound statesmanship. The governments of Europe, with the
single exception of the Emperor of Russia, were
delighted at the prospective downfall of free
government, and sought opportunity and pretext
to take part in its destruction and share in its
spoils. A navy had to be built, arms provided,
and, in fact, every thing necessary to convert a
peaceable, unarmed nation into a vast military
power was to be done, and done quickly. To
accomplish all this, a sum of money was to be
provided and expended, in comparison with
which the revenues and wealth of King Solomon
were but a pittance. Such was the task which
fell upon Mr. Lincoln, and upon men laboring
under his authority. He carried with him into
his labors not only a hopeful heart, but a constitution of iron strength and endurance. Both

were needed, and both were taxed to the utmost by these diversified and urgent cares.

The first battles of the war resulted disastrously to the Union armies. After vast preparations, and with confident hopes of victory, the first battle was fought at Bull Run, resulting in a most disgraceful defeat and rout of the Union troops, who fled frantically back upon Washington. Under this and the great disasters which afterward occurred, Mr. Lincoln bore up with unfailing faith in his cause and confidence in its success. When the tide turned, and victory followed victory in resplendent succession, he did not suffer himself to be unduly exalted or jubilant. Hopeful in disaster, humble in triumph, laborious at all times, he worked out the mission appointed for him of God.

CHAPTER XII.

MR. LINCOLN AND SLAVERY.

DURING the first year and a half of the war, the policy of the Government was to conciliate the pro-slavery element both North and South. Mr. Lincoln was careful to show that he respected the rights guaranteed to slavery by the Constitution. Pro-slavery generals were placed in command. McDowell, Patterson, McClellan, Buell, and others announced that they would not only respect property in slaves, but *assist in putting down an insurrection of slaves against the rebels!* Rebels' horses and corn were to be confiscated, while they were to be aided in retaining their bond *men.* Slaveholders impudently entered the Union armies to search for their lost human chattels. The Hutchinson Family of minstrels volunteered to cheer the soldiers in the Army of the Poto-

mac with their heart-easing songs. One of these,
by the patriot poet Whittier, was as follows:

> What gives the wheat-fields blades of steel?
> What points the rebel cannon?
> What sets the roaring rabble's heel
>   On the old Star-Spangled pennon?
>   What breaks the oath
>   Of the men o' the South?
>   What whets the knife
>   For the Union's life?
> Hark to the answer: SLAVERY!
>
> Then waste no blows on lesser foes
>   In strife unworthy freemen;
> God lifts the veil to-day and shows
>   The features of the demon!
>   O, North and South,
>   Its victims both,
>   Can ye not cry,
>   Let slavery die,
> And Union find in freedom?
>
> What though the cast-out spirit tear
>   The nation in his going?
> We who have shared his guilt must share
>   The pangs of his o'erthrowing.
>   Whate'er the loss,
>   Whate'er the cross,
>   Shall they complain
>   Of present pain
> Who trust in God's hereafter?

For giving voice to these beautiful and heroic lines, General McClellan ordered the Hutchinsons to be expelled at once from the army, and it was done. The liberty-loving people were indignant and clamorous. General Butler eluded the pro-slavery influence by declaring the slaves contraband of war, and, therefore, liable to confiscation—confiscation, of course, meaning emancipation. Generals Hunter and Fremont broke over the restraint and issued emancipating proclamations of their own, and were both removed from command for so doing. But as defeat·followed defeat, and disaster trod upon the bloody heels of disaster, the cry came forth, "LET MY PEOPLE GO!" To every just mind the alternative was not only obvious but the result near at hand—justice or total national destruction. A year and a half was spent in this useless strife against God and the rebels, when the Proclamation of Emancipation sounded clear and strong over the nation. Then the Sun of Righteousness broke upon the land in victory and justice.

How shall the sincerity and integrity of Mr. Lincoln's character be reconciled with his tolerance of such a course on the part of his subalterns? He was one of the first American

7

statesmen to announce that there was an irrepressible mortal conflict between slavery and
freedom—one or the other *must* perish. As we
have seen, before his election he had declared,
with tearful earnestness, " God cares, and humanity cares, and *I care*, and with God's help
I shall not fail." On his journey to Washington to assume the Presidency, in his speech
delivered at Philadelphia, alluding to the principle of the Declaration of Independence, he
said: "If this country can not be saved without
giving up that principle, I would rather be as-
sassinated on the spot than to surrender it."
"I have said nothing but what I am willing to
live by, *and, in the pleasure of Almighty God, to
die by.*" He had from childhood hated and
fought against oppression; and now that slavery
had lifted its knife against the heart of the
nation, this double crime must have intensified
his hatred of it, as it did the abhorrence of
every just man in the civilized world. The facts
will show that Mr. Lincoln did not design that
slavery should live ; that he did not renounce
for an hour his conviction, long before expressed,
that slavery or liberty must perish, utterly and
forever, from the country.

He found, in looking about for the means to resist and destroy the rebellion, that the utmost prudence and caution would be requisite to unite the remaining strength of the nation against it. The great Democratic party was, as such, pro-slavery—a large part of it so much so as to side with and strive, by any means in their power, to secure the triumph of the rebellion. The Republican party, which had elected him, were but half-hearted in their opposition to it. Had he issued his Proclamation of Emancipation any time during the year 1861, the Democrats would have almost unanimously refused further part in the struggle, unless to go in a body to the other side. The border States, then fully half for the Government, would have become as intensely rebellious as South Carolina. So powerful was the pro-slavery influence, even in the party organized to oppose it, that the Republican journals and leaders, during the first eighteen months of the war, indignantly denied that the abolition of slavery formed any part of their motives for prosecuting hostilities; and had the rebels, at any moment during that time, signified their willingness to return to the Union with slavery unimpaired, public opinion, in all parties, would have compelled the Government to receive them. To have adopted radical measures against slavery in rebellion before the public mind was educated to the necessity of so doing, would have proved destructive of the cause of emancipation and of the Republic itself. Just and wise men, who clearly saw the end of the struggle from the beginning and confidently predicted the destruction of slavery, were alarmed at the possibility that Mr. Lincoln, after all, might yield to temporizing expediency and betray the cause of justice, and by betraying, indefinitely delay it; but their fears were groundless. It was acknowledged by those very men that Mr. Lincoln's course was the best course by which the result, so long and so earnestly desired and prayed for, could have been accomplished. God's hand directed the cause of emancipation, and when the hour of destiny came, Abraham Lincoln, with a willing hand, struck the fatal blow; and the death struggles of that mightiest system of wickedness that the world ever saw was visible to all beholders. Mr. Lincoln's policy was not dilatory, not temporizing, but wisely patient in abiding the propitious moment. When the proclamation was directed against the institution it did not fall short, as feebly hurled by the arm of one man, but went crashing to the heart of the mail-clad monster, driven by the mighty power of a united and an indignant nation.*

In a conversation with George Thompson, the distinguished English abolitionist, Mr. Lincoln thus expressed himself: "It is my conviction that had the Proclamation [of Emancipation] been issued even six months earlier than it was, public sentiment would not have sustained it. Just so as to the subsequent enlistment of the blacks in the border States. The step, taken sooner, could not, in my judgment, have been carried out. A man watches his pear-tree, day after day, impatient for the ripening of the fruit. Let him attempt to force the process, and he may spoil both fruit and tree. But let him pa-

---

* In a conversation with a committee of clergymen from Chicago, after he had his proclamation written, they not knowing his intentions, urged the necessity of liberating the slaves, Mr. Lincoln said: "I do not want to issue a document that all the world will see must necessarily be inoperative, like the Pope's bull against the comet," adding, "Whatever shall appear to be God's will, that I will do."

tiently *wait*, and the ripe pear at length falls into his lap. I can now solemnly assert that I have a clear conscience in regard to my action on this momentous question."

Who can doubt this? And yet it must be admitted that the delay was unnecessarily protracted. The people were in advance of their honest, true-hearted Lincoln. The pear was ripe before it fell.

CHAPTER XIII.

HIS RELIGIOUS CHARACTER.

NE of the most beautiful moral specta-
cles to be found upon earth is that of a
Christian wife and mother. Her heart
softened in a Savior's love, her faith reaching beyond the valley, her gentle hand leading the little
ones to the God who gave them, adding sweet-
ness to childish joy, soothing childish sorrow,
enshrined in a husband's love, she is the central object of all that is purest and sweetest in
human society. She gathers to herself the
deepest and strongest affections of the human
heart. Even the hardened and the depraved,
the lost to every other noble emotion are hushed
into respect in her presence. Her influence,
strong in life, grows stronger when her quiet
hands lie moldering in the grave. We cherish
the memory of her loving life, her words, her

assiduous affection, her advice and instruction, as we do no other treasures that lie within the grasp of the mind. How often have those who resisted her influence while she yet lived, and rushed madly down the broad track to destruction, been arrested in their career by a mother who long since passed away and has been forgotten by the world!

As no position can be more elevated and honorable, so none entails responsibilities more profound. The Bible impresses this truth with great clearness, and history continues to verify it in ever-recurring pages. Lincoln's mother had been called to her rest when her little son was scarcely ten years old, and yet his character was formed and his course in life fixed and bounded. He left her hand true to his destiny as the arrow from the hand of the trusty archer. Almost unseen and unknown in that isolated cabin, she clothed his arm with those mighty principles of Christian truth with which she smote the chains from millions of slaves and rescued an imperiled country. And thus, could we trace to their origin the great and noble deeds which here and there light up the history of our race, nearly all would be found due to impressions received in childhood. Nancy Lincoln knew nothing of profound ethical or political principles. The history and science which lay outside of the lids of her Bible were in regions of thought where she had never trod; and yet as a *Christian* she possessed knowledge and moral power for good greater than the learning of the universities could, without this knowledge, afford.

The Bible is so replete with precious promises to Christian parents, and these promises are so often, against apparent probabilities, fulfilled, that the *truly faithful* parent may lay hold of them with perfect assurance. It is even a cause for hope when the object of these prayers and labors has passed to his account.

It has been said that if Lincoln's life and character do not furnish evidence that he was a Christian, we may look in vain for such evidences anywhere among men. Secretary Seward said: "He is the best man I ever knew." Dr. Bellows, who knew him intimately, said: "He is the purest-hearted man I ever knew." The people know him to have been marked with more humility than any man they ever elected to high office. No man since Cromwell (and we doubt the justice of excepting him) so entirely

distrusted his own ability to meet future emergencies, or so wholly disclaimed the glory of past
triumphs by referring all to the beneficent power
and providence of God. "I should be the most
presumptuous blockhead upon this footstool," he
once said, "if I for one day thought that I could
discharge the duties which have come upon me
since I came to this place, without the aid and
enlightenment of One who is stronger and wiser
than all others."

And yet had he glided quietly down the stream
of life, he would have been regarded as a man
full of generous virtues, of high-toned and inflexible morality, but not a Christian. It required
the tremendous ordeal through which he passed,
like the refiner's fire, to consume the dross and
bring forth the fine gold. It is possible to be
very near the kingdom of God, and yet lack one
thing needful. If he had truly consecrated himself to the Lord Jesus before that trial of his
faith came, the probabilities are strong that he
would have openly and publicly professed his
name and acknowledged his claims. The Savior
has made it a duty to unite with his visible
church. Greater duties than that may be vio-
lated by a man who is truly a disciple of Christ,

and yet it is not the neglect of duty alone in this particular which gives it its weight in determining Christian character. The fellowship of the saints is the natural element of the converted man. He is impelled by his wants and desires to seek their companionship and communion. When the man's heart is warmed by the love of Jesus, he wants every other man to love Jesus, and will do all he can to impart his joy to others. He thirsts for more light and knowledge on this absorbing interest, and hears with avidity the Christian experience of Christian people.

Nothing of all this is seen in Lincoln's life until shortly before his first election to the Presidency. With a grasp of intellect which our ablest statesmen do not seem to have possessed, he had seized upon the character of slavery, the relations it bore to the will and attributes of Almighty God, the immense power in which it was intrenched, and from these facts and the signs of the times was convinced that the tremendous contest was near at hand. He knew intellectually that "our God is a mighty tower," and then, as we believe, and as he himself thought, it was that he first earnestly desired security within its impregnable walls.

It may be asked, How could a man think *more* upon the subjects of God's justice and providence, and the desirableness of faith in Christ *than upon all others* for years, and yet have no love for God? What hidden motive would impel him to carry the Testament in his bosom, and how could he truly describe it as his rock without having *felt* its shadows above his head and its firm footing beneath his feet? Does any man habitually for years employ a large proportion of his thoughts upon God's perfections and providence unless he loves God? We may not know that dividing line which is known only to the Father of spirits; yet "no man lighteth a candle and putteth it under a bushel." "My sheep hear my voice, and they know me and they follow me. He that confess-eth me before men him will I confess before my Father." God knows our time and our future, and in his own good time and way brings his saints into his kingdom.

Mr. Lincoln once asked a lady connected with the Christian Commission for her idea of true Christian experience. " Mrs. ——," said he, " I have formed a high opinion of your Christian character, and now, as we are alone, I wish you, in brief, to give me your idea of what constitutes a true religious experience." The lady replied that, in her judgment, "it consisted of a conviction of one's own sinfulness and weakness, and personal need of the Savior for strength and support; and that when one was brought to feel his need of Divine help, and to seek daily the aid of the Holy Spirit for strength and guidance, it was satisfactory evidence of his having been born again." Mr. Lincoln replied, earnestly : "If this is really a correct view of this great subject, I think I can say, with sincerity, that I hope I am a Christian. * * I think I can safely say that I know something of that *change* of which you speak; and I will further add, that it has been my intention for some time, at a suitable opportunity, to make a public religious profession."

Afterward, referring to a change of heart, he said he could not mention any particular period when he experienced such a change, except so far that he thought it became manifest to him at the period of his first election to the Presidency, and that in the crisis immediately following, his mind became more confident and fixed upon this subject.

In a conversation with Hon. H. C. Deming, of Connecticut, he said: "I have not united myself to any church, because I have found difficulty in giving my assent, without mental reservation, to the long-complicated statements of Christian doctrine which characterize their articles of belief and confessions of faith. When any church will inscribe over its altar the Savior's condensed statement of both law and gospel, 'Thou shalt love the Lord thy God with all thy heart, and with all thy soul, and with all thy mind, and thy neighbor as thyself,' that church will I join with all my heart and with all my soul."

A clergyman, who, if his expression correctly indicated his feelings, must have been a doubting Thomas, once remarked to Lincoln that he "hoped the Lord was *on our side* in this contest." The reply was as characteristic as it was epigrammatic and noble: "I am not at all concerned about that," said he, "for I know the Lord *is always on the side of the right;* but it is my constant prayer and anxiety that *I* and *this nation* should be *on the Lord's side.*" That sentence contains the kernel and essence of all true statesmanship.

Let us trace Mr. Lincoln's Christian character by the light of other events. Armies, both as such and as individuals, have always been prone to disregard the obligations of the Sabbath. This gave Mr. Lincoln great pain. So much was his feelings enlisted by the wanton violations of the Lord's day, that on the 16th of November, 1863, he issued a circular, saying: " The importance for man and beast of the prescribed weekly rest, the sacred rights of Christian soldiers and sailors, a becoming deference to the best sentiment of a Christian people, and a due regard for the Divine will, demand that Sunday labor in the army and navy be reduced to the measure of strict necessity. * * The discipline of the national forces should not suffer, nor the cause they defend be imperiled, by the profanation of the *name* or the *day* of the Most High." We need not allude to the joyous proclamations of thanksgiving sounded forth by him at various times when God gave us victory, because the rebel chief blasphemously sought, by similar proclamations, to implicate God in his burnings and butcheries for the establishment of slavery; and we have, within a brief period after his departure, heard devout proclamations from lips foul with falsehood and odorous from the carousal; but we know that from him they were the outburst of emotion from a sincerely-thankful heart.

When the great battle of Stone River was in progress, Mr. Lincoln was informed of it, and became so anxious that he could not eat. A lady friend told him that he must trust in God, and at least could pray. "Yes," he said, "I can," and, taking up his Bible, left the room. The news of the rout of Bragg soon followed, and Lincoln came in, exclaiming, "Good news! Good news! The victory is ours, and God is good." "Nothing like praying," said the lady. "Yes, there is," said Lincoln—"PRAISE—prayer, *and* praise."

In February, 1862, he lost a little son, in whose life his affections were bound up by the tenderest ties of parental love—little WILLIE. His loss afflicted Mr. Lincoln deeply. A Christian lady told him the people were praying for him. "I am glad to hear that," he said; "I want them to pray for me; I need their prayers;' and added, "I will try to go to God with my sorrows." Afterward he said: "I think I can trust in God; I wish I had that childlike faith you speak of, and I think God will give it to me." What language could be more childlike in faith than this?

We select illustrations without regard to chronological order. A few members of the Christian Commission, in whose labors he took unflagging interest, in conversing with him one day, referred to the trust they could repose in God's providence. Mr. Lincoln replied: "If it were not for my firm belief in an overruling Providence, it would be difficult for me, in such a complication of affairs, to keep my reason on its seat. But I am confident that the Almighty has his plans and will work them out. * * I have always taken counsel of him, and referred to him my plans, and have never adopted a course of proceeding without being assured, as far as I could be, of his approbation."

Mr. Lincoln had a supreme contempt for hypocrisy in religion, and many were the times, in his professional career as a lawyer and a politician, that he subjected it to his merciless ridicule. Of this we give a single illustration. The wife of a rebel officer, imprisoned on Johnson's Island, beset him for his release, alledging that her husband was a "*very religious man!*" Mr.

Lincoln could not but be touched with the ridiculous nature of this appeal, and said: "Tell him that, in my opinion, the religion that sets men to fight and rebel against their Government because, as they think, that Government does not sufficiently help them to eat *their* bread in the sweat of *other men's* faces, is not the sort of religion upon which men can get to heaven."

We may further trace the religious tendencies and character of Lincoln's mind by his literary preferences. In a conversation with Mr. F. B. Carpenter,* the artist, he remarked: "There are some quaint, queer verses, written, I think, by Oliver W. Holmes, entitled 'The Last Leaf,' one of which is to me inexpressibly touching; it is this:

> "The mossy marbles rest
>   On the lips that he has pressed
>   In their bloom,
>   And the names he loved to hear
>   Have been carved for many a year
>   On the tomb!"

---

* Mr. Carpenter was employed, for a period of six months, in producing his great picture, "The First Reading of the Emancipation Proclamation," during which time he was on intimate relations with Lincoln. He has since produced a book of extraordinary interest, "Six Months at the White House," to which we are indebted for the above, and also for some incidents hereinafter related.

"For pure pathos," said he, "there is nothing finer than these six lines in the English language."

His "favorite poem," now so widely known, he clipped from the columns of a newspaper while a young man, and by frequent readings came to know it by heart. It was written by William Knox, a young man who died in Edinburgh, Scotland, in 1825. This poem Mr. Lincoln recited to friends at various times. It is as follows:

WHY SHOULD THE SPIRIT OF MORTAL BE PROUD?

O, why should the spirit of mortal be proud?
Like a swift-flying meteor, fast-flying cloud,
A flash of the lightning, a break of the wave,
He passes from life to his rest in his grave.

The leaves of the oak and the willow shall fade,
Be scattered abroad and together be laid,
And the young and the old, and the low and the high,
Shall molder to dust, and together shall lie.

The infant a mother attended and loved,
The mother that infant's affection who proved,
The husband that mother and infant who blessed,
Each, all are away to their dwelling of rest.

The maid on whose cheek, on whose brow, in whose eye
Shone beauty and pleasure, her triumphs are by;

And the memory of those who loved her and praised
Are alike from the minds of the living erased.

The hand of the king that the scepter hath borne,
The brow of the priest that the miter hath worn,
The eye of the sage and the heart of the brave,
Are hidden and lost in the depths of the grave.

The peasant whose lot was to sow and to reap,
The herdsman who climbed with his goats up the steep,
The beggar who wandered in search of his bread,
Have faded away like the grass that we tread.

The saint who enjoyed the communion of heaven,
The sinner who dared to remain unforgiven,
The wise and the foolish, the guilty and just,
Have quietly mingled their bones in the dust.

So the multitude go, like the flower or the weed
That withers away to let others succeed:
So the multitude come, even there we behold,
To respect every tale that has often been told.

For we are the same that our fathers have been;
We see the same sights that our fathers have seen;
We drink the same stream, we view the same sun,
And run the same course our fathers have run.

The thoughts we are thinking, our fathers would think;
From the death we are shrinking, our fathers would
    shrink;
To the life we are clinging, they also would cling,
But it speeds from us all like a bird on the wing.

They loved—but the story we can not unfold;
They scorned—but the heart of the haughty is cold;
They grieved—but no wail from their slumber will come;
They joyed—but the tongue of their gladness is dumb.

They died—ah, they died! We things that are now,
That walk on the turf that lies over their brow,
And make in their dwellings a transient abode,
Meet the things that they met on their pilgrimage road.

Yea, hope and despondency, pleasure and pain,
Are mingled together in sunshine and rain,
And the smile and the tear, the song and the dirge,
Still follow each other, like surge upon surge.

'T is the wink of an eye, 't is the draught of a breath,
From the blossom of health to the paleness of death,
From the gilded saloon to the bier and the shroud—
O, why should the spirit of mortal be proud!

Mr. Lincoln *never read a novel.* He said he once began to read "Ivanhoe," but cast it aside. A single one of those books of delusive dreams might have, in early life, tempted his mind from the difficult facts and problems of life, and led him to waste his energies in regions of idle imagination and sickly fancy.

While he probably had no fear of becoming a drunkard, he was careful not to take the *first step* in that direction, being a *temperate* man in the ·only true sense of that term, *total absti-nence.*

The prevalence of drinking habits in high places at Washington are well known. Every office, from that of President to the lowest, has at one time or another been disgraced by an incumbent possessed with the ruinous and. degrading vice. Mr. Lincoln was, in consequence, often pressed to take a "social glass," but always refused. The *Religious Telescope*, published at Dayton, Ohio, in its issue of June 19th, 1867, relates the following, which may serve as an example of many similar incidents which might be related :

" Mr. Lincoln is well known to have been a man of rigid temperance principles. A circumstance illustrating his habits in this respect is worthy of repetition here. During his first presidential campaign he made a speech in the city of Dayton. A prominent citizen invited him to drink before speaking, that he might have the benefit of a warmer circulation. He declined the proffered courtesy, saying, 'I never drink, sir.' He then added : 'You remember that Douglas and I stumped Illinois together. He drank every day, and I did n't drink at all. He broke down, and I did n't.' "

He might personally have been safe in making concessions to the drinking usages of the times, but he felt that he had no right to endanger the bodies and souls of others by such an example. It was his duty, as it is the duty of every young man, to manifest his independence and manhood by standing upon principle, and yielding not an iota to usages and customs and such claims of etiquette as require him to do wrong. The drinking-cup, the social game of cards, the billiard-table, the lottery—he who yields to such amusements unmans and degrades himself to that extent. We are proud of our political liberties. Let us be equally jealous of any weakness on our own part, or influence upon us by others, that may render us the weak, contemptible, unmanly slaves of vice.

CHAPTER XIV.

INSTANCES OF PATIENCE.

PROBABLY no man of prominence in modern times possessed, in such an eminent degree, the power of self-control as Mr. Lincoln. In some persons, evenness of temper arises from insensibility or indifference. The slings and arrows which goad other men to passion or grief rebound harmlessly from their insensate armor, not attracting serious notice. In such persons forbearance is not a virtue, because it does not arise from principle but from a want of feeling. Mr. Lincoln was, as we have seen, sensitive, and susceptible both to pleasure and pain; yet he was rarely, if ever, provoked to personal recrimination or revenge.

It is probable that the severest, because most protracted, test of his patience and forbearance arose from his relations with General McClellan. Without wishing unnecessarily to discuss this

general's character, it is sufficient to say that he
was pro-slavery in his political opinions, and
held his military skill and his statesmanship in
much higher estimation than his countrymen
have since done. Delaying for weary months,
at the head of the finest army in the world, in
supine inaction, he treated Mr. Lincoln's urgent
appeals for vigorous effort with contempt and
often with insolence. When his army was wast-
ing in his ill-fated peninsular campaign, he busied
himself in writing pretentious instructions to the
President in regard to his proper policy; all of
which he knew to be contrary to the views of
the Cabinet, and which, had they been complied
with, would have proved as disastrous to the
country as his own military management was
to his army. Reaching the climax of insolent
effrontery, he wrote a letter charging the President with conspiring to destroy the army of
which he was commander. Any other Commander-in-chief would have instantly ordered
his removal and trial by court-martial. Lincoln
sought only that in McClellan's course which he
could commend, wrote to him frequently the
most encouraging letters, deferred against his
own judgment to McClellan's so-called "strat-

egy,' and only removed him when convinced, as the country had long previously been, of his unfitness for the command. After McClellan's removal, Lincoln expressed his desire to find some post for him, where whatever engineering ability he might possess could be employed.

General McClellan was nominated by the pro-slavery party, in 1864, in opposition to Mr. Lincoln. The result was Lincoln's overwhelming triumph before the people. One would suppose it impossible for him to achieve this triumph, over one who had so denounced him, without exultation. When a delegation of friends called upon to congratulate him, he said:

"I am thankful to God for this approval of the people. But, while deeply grateful for this mark of confidence in me, if I know my heart, my gratitude is free from any taint of personal triumph. I do not impugn the motives of any one opposed to me. It is no pleasure to me to triumph over any one, but I give thanks to Almighty God for this evidence of the people's resolution to stand by the Government and the rights of humanity."

The re-nomination of Mr. Lincoln for the Presidency in 1864 called forth a storm of abuse and calumny such as had fallen upon the good name of no previous candidate. He was constantly and habitually referred to by his opponents as the "tyrant," the "widow-maker," "butcher," "beast," "baboon," and "monster." He was described as avaricious, blood-thirsty, and cruel; and every effort was made to convince the people that his efforts to destroy the rebellion were, in reality, made to supplant republican institutions by a monarchy, with himself as the autocrat. These false accusations and vile epithets were intended to destroy confidence in the Union cause, and to weaken and defeat the Union armies. But Mr. Lincoln never noticed them, in word or deed, nor harbored a thought of retaliation or revenge.

In full view of all these attempted injuries to himself, with all the malice, treachery, cruelty, and unexampled barbarity of the rebellion, amid the exasperating and hardening circumstances of fierce civil war, his second inaugural sincerely expressed the emotions of his heart: "With malice toward none, with charity for all, with firmness for the right, as God gives us to see the right, let us strive on to finish the work we are in; to bind up the nation's wounds; to

care for him who shall have borne the battle,
and for his widow and his orphan; to do all
which may achieve and cherish a just and
lasting peace among ourselves and with all
nations."

The point of character in which he was supposed to be most deficient was that of firmness
in the administration of penal justice. That he
erred on the side of clemency is probably true,
and yet that there was any of that contemptible
mawkish sympathy for atrocious criminals, when
brought to justice, which of late so paralyzes
the defensive arm of the law, is not true. While
he could remain calm and unruffled under the
most exasperating abuse and injury of himself,
injustice and villainy inflicted upon *others* inva-
riably aroused his indignation—not a mere ebul-
lition of feeling, but the hostility which mani-
fests itself in *deeds*. During his administration
we had none of the wholesale pardons of coun-
terfeiters, and murderers, and traitors which
indifference to crime prompted in his immediate
successor. On the contrary, no gross or sordid
crime escaped the appropriate penalty, during
his administration, through any culpable tender-
ness on his part.

A slave-trader who had been sentenced to five years' imprisonment in the penitentiary of Massachusetts, and a fine of one thousand dollars, had served his full time in the state-prison, but could not pay his fine so as to obtain release. A very strong appeal was made on his behalf by some respectable, namby-pamby people of that State.   Mr. Lincoln read the document, and then said to the messenger: "My friend, that is very touching.   You know my weakness is to be, if possible, too easily moved by appeals for mercy, and if this man were guilty of the foulest murder, I might forgive him on such an appeal; but the man who could go to Africa and rob her of her children, and sell them into interminable bondage, with no other motive than that which is furnished by dollars and cents, is so much worse than the most depraved murderer, that he can never receive pardon at my hands.   No, he may rot in jail before he shall have liberty by any act of mine."

The heartless oppressor, the mercenary robber, the cool, calculating criminal of any sort, might as well appeal to a blind statue of Justice as to him.   But the wearied sentinel, overcome with sleep upon his beat; the deserter; even the rebel spy, who took his life in his hand for a bad cause, and persons guilty of other acts in themselves criminal, if the result of sudden temptation or passion, found in him a merciful magistrate.

A boy who fell asleep while on guard in the Army of the Potomac, was sentenced to be shot. On the presentation of the warrant for his signature, Mr. Lincoln said: "It is not a wonder that a boy raised on a farm, and probably in the habit of going to bed at dark, should fall asleep while required to watch. I can not consent that he should be shot for such an act. I should regard the blood of the poor young man as on my skirts." This young man was found with the slain on the field of Fredericksburg, with a photograph of Mr. Lincoln next his heart, upon which was written, "God bless Mr. Lincoln."

A number of deserters, twenty-four, were sentenced at one time to death, and the military authorities insisted that the discipline of the army would be ruined if Mr. Lincoln pardoned them. He replied: "Mr. General, there are too many weeping widows already in the United States. For God's sake, do not ask me to add to their number, for I WON'T DO IT!"

When the notorious guerrilla ("horse-thief," as Parson Brownlow always called him) John Morgan was killed, some one brought the news to Mr. Lincoln. "Well," said he, "I would not crow over anybody's death, but I can take Morgan's death as resignedly as I can anybody's." Pausing a moment, he indignantly exclaimed: "Morgan was a coward and a negro-driver—the kind of a man that the North knows nothing about."

A friend and neighbor of Judge Kellogg, of Illinois, who had enlisted, was guilty of a misdemeanor, for which he was tried by court-martial and condemned to be shot. The night previous to the day on which he was to be executed, Kellogg heard of it, and applied to the Secretary of War for a reprieve. Stanton flatly refused. "Too much leniency in the service already; we must make an example of him." "Well," Mr. Secretary," said Kellogg, "I give you fair notice that *the boy is not going to be shot.*" So saying, he posted off to Lincoln, who had retired for the night, and partly begged, partly forced his way into Lincoln's sleeping-room. The President listened quietly to the excited Congressman, and then, rising on his elbow, said : " Well, I do n't believe *shooting him* will do him any good; give me that pen."

A boy soldier was confined at Elmira, New York, and under sentence of death for the atrocious crime of poisoning his guards, who were at the time holding him in confinement for desertion. One of the guards died from the effects of the poison. His mother and other friends made repeated efforts to have the sentence commuted, without avail. On the morning of the day when the prisoner was to die, his friends succeeded in convincing Lincoln that he was probably insane. He at once ordered a reprieve till this question could be determined; and greatly fearing his telegraphic dispatch should fail to reach Elmira in time to save the boy's life, sent, during the forenoon, three other dispatches by as many different lines to different parties at Elmira, each repeating the reprieve.

A poor girl, a foreigner, whose only friend was a brother in the army, received the crushing intelligence that her brother had been induced to desert, and was captured and condemned. She went to Washington, and tried, without avail, to get an interview with the President. Hon. Thomas Ford, of Ohio, met her at the portico of the White House, and his sympathies were deeply enlisted. As he had an appointment to meet the President, he told her to follow him closely, and force herself between him and the President, and present her plea. She did as she was instructed. Lincoln looked first at her tearful face, then at her neat but scanty dress, and said: "My poor girl, you have come here with no governor or senator to plead your cause. You seem honest and truthful, and—*you do n't wear hoops*, and I will be whipped but I will pardon your brother."

This pardoning of deserters was just as well as humane. Young men and boys who were in the ranks, and whose relations were besotted with the virus of slavery, were, during the whole of the war, discouraged, deceived, and induced to desert by their traitorous friends at home. The pardoning power, so freely used, saved the life of many a young man who was less to blame for desertion than the unprincipled people who thus covertly and basely sought to weaken the armies and destroy the Government.

A poor woman, advanced in life, obtained an interview with the President, and said: "My husband and three sons all went into the army.

9

My husband was killed at the fight at ——. I got along very badly since then, living all alone, and I thought I would come and ask you to release to me my oldest son." Mr. Lincoln replied, in his kindest tone, "Certainly, certainly, my good woman, if you have given us *all*, and your prop has been taken away, you are justly entitled to one of your boys." The poor woman thanked him gratefully, and, fearing to trust her precious paper to other hands, went with it herself to the front in search of her son. She found him in a hospital mortally wounded. Having buried him, she returned with a broken heart to the President. He was greatly affected by her appearance and story, and said : "I know what you wish me to do, and I will do it without your asking." He then took up a pen and commenced writing an order for the release of the second son. "While he was writing, the poor woman stood by his side, the tears running down her face, and passed her hand softly over his head, stroking his rough hair as I have seen a fond mother caress a son. By the time he had finished writing, his own eyes and heart were full. He handed her the paper : 'Now,' said he, '*you* have one and *I* one of the other two left; that is no more than right.' She took the paper, and reverently placing her hand again upon his head, the tears still upon her cheeks, said : 'The Lord bless you, Mr. Lincoln. May you live a thousand years, and may you always be the head of this great nation!'"

"A couple of well-known New York gentlemen called upon the President to solicit a pardon for a man who, while acting as mate for a sailing vessel, had struck one of his men a blow which resulted in his death. Convicted and sentenced for manslaughter, a powerful appeal was made in his behalf, as he had previously borne a good character. Giving the facts a hearing, Mr. Lincoln responded :

"'Well, gentlemen, leave your papers, and I will have the Attorney-General, Judge Bates, look them over, and we will see what can be done. Being both of us *pigeon-hearted* fellows, the chances are that, if there is any ground whatever for interference, the scoundrel will get off!'" *

Instances similar to the preceding were constantly recurring during the last eventful years of Mr. Lincoln's life. They were a source of

---

* "Six Months at the White House."

pleasure and rest to him. He said, in referring
to his free exercise of the pardoning power,
"Some of our generals complain that I impair
discipline and subordination in the army by my
pardons and respites; but it makes me rested
after a hard day's work, if I can find a good
excuse for saving a man's life, and I go to bed
happy, as I think how joyous the signing of my
name will make him and his family and friends."

That was a prescription for securing a good
night's sleep which it would be well for us all to
adopt. The reflection that we have during the
day carried joy to some one's heart, and have
sincerely sought to fulfill our duty toward God
and our neighbors, is well calculated to tranquil-
ize our minds and bring softly upon our closing
eyes the balmy shades of slumber.

CHAPTER XV.

LINCOLN STORIES—A REMARKABLE TRAIT.

"DO you think my father has gone to heaven?" asked little Tad. Lincoln of a gentleman who called upon the family when their great sorrow had fallen upon them. "I have not a doubt of it," was the reply. "Then I am *glad* he has gone there," said the boy, in accents broken with sobbing, "for he never was happy after he came here. This was not a good place for him."

A lady who was urging the establishment of hospitals in the Northern States, to which sick and wounded soldiers might be brought, described the suffering of the invalids in the comfortless field hospitals in the South, and added, "If you will grant my petition, it will make you happy as long as you live." With countenance betraying extreme dejection and pain, the

President replied : "Not *happy. I shall never be happy any more.*"

In conversing with his wife, a few hours before his decease, he said : "We must be more cheerful in the future ; between the war and the loss of our darling Willie we have been *very miserable.*"

And yet this man, burdened with a nation's sorrows, will pass into history as the most inveterate joker of his time. He presented the strange anomaly of a mind naturally yielding to sadness and melancholy, and yet possessing the liveliest appreciation of wit and humor. When weariness and care pressed too heavily upon him, he was able to make a quick transition to the other extreme. The furrowed face, every line of which was full of sadness, would suddenly break from the gloomy shadows and light up with mirth. When a good story was gotten off, and a hearty laugh indulged, he returned as suddenly to his toil and habitual sadness. The stories were always for a specific purpose, and from the relaxation and rest they afforded him, as the following examples will show :

" Violent criticism, attacks, and denunciation, coming either from radicals or conservatives, rarely ruffled the President, if they reached his ears. It was in connection with something of this kind that he told me this story: 'Some years ago,' said he, 'a couple of emigrants fresh from the 'Emerald Isle,' seeking labor, were making their way toward the West. Coming suddenly, one evening, upon a pond of water, they were greeted with a grand chorus of bull-frogs, a kind of music they had never heard be-fore: 'Breck-eck-ex, B-a-u-m, B-a-u-m.' Over-come with terror, they clutched their shillalahs, and crept cautiously forward, straining their eyes in every direction to catch sight of the 'inemy,' but he was not to be found! At last a happy idea seized the foremost one; he sprang to his companion and exclaimed, 'And sure, Jamie, it's my opinion that it's nothing but a *noise!*' "

Some Western tourists, who had called on the President, referred to the picturesque names given by the Indians to many localities, streams, and other natural objects, referring, among oth-ers, to the " Weeping Water " in Nebraska. Mr. Lincoln, looking up, replied: " As 'Laugh-ing Water,' according to Longfellow, is 'Minne-haha,' this evidently should be *Minneboohoo!*"

A farmer called to protest against depredations made by Union soldiers on his hay, horse-feed, etc.; Lincoln told him the following story :

" In my early days, I knew a lumberman in Illinois, one Jack Case, who was one of the best raftsmen on the river. It was quite a trick in those times to take the logs over the rapids, but Jack always kept his raft straight in the channel. Finally, a steamer was put on, and Jack (he's dead now, poor fellow !) was made captain of her. One day, when the boat was plunging and wallowing along the boiling rapids, and Jack's utmost vigilance was exercised to keep her in the narrow channel, a boy pulled his coattail and hailed him with, 'I say, Mr. Captain, I wish you would just stop your boat a minute— *I've lost my apple overboard!*' "

When Porter's great naval expedition against Port Royal sailed out from Hampton Roads, and the country was full of curiosity concerning its destination, an inquisitive patriot called on the President and confidentially asked for the much-coveted information.

"Would you really like to know?" queried the President.

"I am *very* desirous of knowing, Mr. President."

"And will you sacredly promise me to keep the secret if I tell you?"

The anxious inquirer was ready to pledge himself by any amount of sacred and pecuniary obligations.

"Well, then," said Lincoln, "I will tell you," and advancing to the expectant listener, he took him by the coat-collar, placed his lips to his ear, and whispered, with portentous earnestness, "*Porter has gone down South!*"

Another visitor bothered him to know how many men the rebels had in the field. Lincoln replied, gravely, "Twelve hundred thousand!"

"TWELVE HUNDRED THOUSAND!" exclaimed the astonished questioner, with alarm starting from his open mouth and eyes.

"Yes, sir, twelve hundred thousand. You see, all of our generals, when they get whipped, say that the enemy outnumbers them from three or five to one, and I must believe them. We have four hundred thousand men in the field, and *three times four make twelve!* Don't you see it?"

Some croakers were making themselves inter-

esting by prophesying all sorts of ruin and disaster to the cause—"breakers ahead"—"impending crisis," and all that. "That reminds
me," said Lincoln, "of the school-boy who never
could pronounce the names Shadrack, Mesheck,
and Abednego. He had been repeatedly whipped
for it, without effect. Some time afterward, see-
ing the names occur in the regular lesson for
the day, he put his finger upon the place and
whispered to his next neighbor, 'Here comes
those tormented Hebrews again!'"

In one of his debates with Senator Douglas,
the latter had attempted to escape his conclusions by denying the veracity of a senator whom
he had quoted. Lincoln replied that it was not
a question of veracity: "By a course of reasoning," said he, "Euclid proves that all the angles
in a triangle are equal to two right angles.
Now, if you undertake to disprove that proposition, would you prove it to be false *by calling
Euclid a liar?*"

A delegation of ministers made a persevering
and pertinacious effort to induce the President
to correct alledged evils in the appointment of
army chaplains, many of whom, they urged,
were unfit for the position. "But, gentlemen,"

said he, "that is a matter which the Government has nothing to do with; the chaplains are chosen by the regiment." The ministers were not satisfied, but urged a change in the manner of selecting them. Lincoln had his unfailing resource to end the controversy, and resorted to it. "Without any disrespect, gentlemen, I will tell you a 'little story.' Once, in Springfield, I was going off on a short journey, and reached the depot a little ahead of time. Leaning against the fence, just outside the depot, was a little darkey boy whom I knew, named Dick, busily digging with his toe in a mud-puddle. As I came up, I said: 'Dick, what are you about?' 'Making a church,' said he. 'A church!' said I; 'what do you mean?' 'Why, yes,' said Dick, pointing with his toe, 'don't you see? There is the shape of it; there's the steps and front-door, here the pews where the folks set, and there's the pulpit.' 'Yes, I see,' said I; 'but why don't you make a minister?' Laws,' answered Dick, with a grin, 'I ha'n t got *mud* enough!'"

It was known that the rebel traitor Jacob Thompson would make an effort to pass through a Northern State, just after the fall of Richmond, for the purpose of escaping from the country. The Secretary of War urged that he ought to be arrested and punished as a traitor. " Well," said Lincoln, " let me tell you a story. There was an Irish soldier here last summer, who wanted something to drink stronger than water, and stepped into a drug-store, where he espied a soda-fountain. ' Mr. Doctor,' said he, ' give me, if you plase, a glass of soda-wather, and if yees will put in a few draps o' whishkey *unbeknown till me*, I'll be obleeged.' Now," said Lincoln, " if Jake Thompson is permitted to pass through ' unbeknown,' what's the harm? So don't have him arrested."

Speaking of the office-seekers who thronged so incessantly and pertinaciously upon him, he said: " I am like a man so busy in letting rooms in one end of his house, that he can't stop to put out the fire that is burning in the other."

It was intimated to him that Secretary —— would be a formidable rival for succession to the Presidency. With the usual reservation, " meaning no disrespect," he said: " R—, you were brought up on a farm, were you not? Then you know what a *chin-fly* is. Well, my brother and I were once plowing corn on a Kentucky

farm, I driving the horse, he holding the plow.
The horse was lazy, but on one occasion he
rushed across the field so that I could scarcely
keep up with him. On reaching the end of the
furrow, I found an enormous chin-fly fastened
upon him, and knocked it off. My brother
asked what I did that for. I told him I did n't
want the horse bitten in that way. ' Why,'
said my brother, ' *that's all that made him go!* '
Now, if Secretary —— has a presidential *chin-
fly* biting him, I'm not going to knock it off;
it will only make his department *go!* "

As the rebel confederacy was tumbling in its
final crash, Lincoln foresaw the embarrassment
which the capture of Jeff. Davis would bring
upon him, and was asked by a friend what he
was going to do with him. He replied: "There
was a boy in Springfield who saved up his
money and bought a 'coon, which, after the nov-
elty had worn off, became a great nuisance. He
was one day leading him through the street, and
had all he could do to keep clear of the little
vixen, which had torn his clothes half off him.
At last he sat down on a curb-stone, completely
flagged out. A man passing, was stopped by
the disconsolate appearance of the little fellow,

and asked him the matter. ' O," said he, ' this
'coon is such a trouble to me!' ' Why do n't
you get rid of him, then ?' said the gentleman.
' Hush!' said the boy, ' do n't you see he is
gnawing his rope off? I 'm going to let him do
it, and when I go home *I can tell the folks that
he got away from me!* "

He was free to make merry at his own personal appearance. He was dressed for a state
party one evening, and, holding up his gloved
hands, said : " An Illinois friend tells me that
he can never see these without thinking of *can-
vased hams.*"

A friend observing the accuracy of a new
portrait of him, spoke of it in flattering terms.
" Yes," said Lincoln, " it is *horridly* like me ; "
and added : " That reminds me of a good woman,
not remarkable for good looks, who, on a visit to
the Young Men's Christian Association, caught
sight of herself in a concealed looking-glass,
and retired in great confusion, saying she would
not visit an institution where she could not go
without meeting *disreputable* people."

Volumes of such " stories " might be gathered
from the newspapers of the time, which repro-
duced them, from time to time, under the caption

of " Old Abe's Last." Such wit is a valuable
faculty, designed by the beneficent Creator to
add to the happiness of his creatures. The use
of this talent for the purpose of wounding the
sensibilities of our neighbors, or giving them
pain in any manner, is, therefore, a direct per-
version of its use, and a heinous abuse of God's
goodness, and will surely be punished. Cheer-
fulness and merriment are not inconsistent with
Christian character; it is inconsistent only in
those who are " without hope and without God
in the world." The Psalmist, in describing his
inexpressible joy at the return of the people
from captivity, said:

> " When Zion's bondage God turned back,
>   *As men that dreamed were we;*
>   Then filled with *laughter* was our mouth,
>   Our tongues with melody."

If the use of wit and humor for the purpose of
injuring another is directly contrary to the purposes of God in giving the faculty, the use of it
in obscenity and vulgarity is a horrible degra-
dation, fit only for the carnivals of devils. Let
every young man beware of listening to it, as
he prides in his manhood, or hopes for happiness
here or in the world to come. Many a Chris-

tian man is stung in his inmost soul by the recollection that he, at some time in his life, has been guilty of this degrading abuse of his intellectual gifts. Nor is it lawful or consistent with Christian character to use ridicule as a weapon except in *self-defense.* It is a sharp blade if handled by a master. It may be used properly and lawfully in cutting down the pride of scoffers or unprincipled assailants of truth, not against an honest or misled opponent. Him we are bound to convince with truth itself, not to attack and annoy, or humiliate with the superiority of wit.

CHAPTER XVI.

MAGNITUDE OF THE WAR.

IT will be difficult for those who come after us either to realize the vast proportions of the American civil war, or to appreciate the feelings of the people while bearing its burdens. The rescue of the country was undertaken with enthusiasm and alacrity, but with a very limited conception of the immensity of the task. The burden grew gradually heavier as the months of self-sacrifice, toil, and sorrow wore away, until it seemed too heavy to be borne, and yet the President and people sustained it with hopefulness, fortitude, and resolution such as has not been exceeded in the history of man. The debt of the General Government rose, notwithstanding the heaviest practical taxation, to the sum of over twenty-seven hundred millions of dollars; and this did not in-

10

clude nearly all the pecuniary burdens created
by the war. Nearly two and a quarter millions
of soldiers were, from first to last, enlisted in the
service of the Government. Three hundred and
sixty battles were fought upon the land. The
deaths resulting directly and indirectly from the
war, among the Union forces, can never be accu-
rately known, but were probably not less than a
quarter of a million. It is vain to attempt a conception of the physical agony, the sorrow of
friends, and the weight pressing on the hearts
and minds of the people which were endured;
and yet such were the terrible calamities which
arose from that bottomless pit of oppression and
cruelty, American slavery.

Every day of the life of Mr. Lincoln, during
the progress of this contest, was of necessity
crowded with important events and labors. But
there are but a few other incidents which the
limits proposed in this volume will permit to be
noticed. These are selected as showing at once
his character and his style as a writer and con-
troversialist.

When the battle of Antietam was in progress,
he made a solemn vow to God that if he would
give us the victory, he would free the bondmen

in our land; that he would take this as an indication that the time had come to execute this
act of justice. On the 17th of September that
battle was fought and won; on the 22d, the preliminary Proclamation of Emancipation was
issued, declaring that "on the first day of January, in the year of our Lord, 1863, all persons
held as slaves within any State, or designated
part of a State, the people whereof shall then be
in rebellion against the United States, SHALL BE
THEN, THENCEFORWARD, AND FOREVER FREE."

On the first day of January, in accordance
with this · proclamation, he issued its counter-
part: "I do order and declare that all persons
held as slaves within said designated States and
parts of States ARE AND HENCEFORWARD SHALL
BE FREE, and that the Executive Government
of the United States, including the military and
naval authorities thereof, will RECOGNIZE AND
MAINTAIN the freedom of said persons.

"And I hereby enjoin upon the people so declared to be free to abstain from all violence,
unless in necessary self-defense; and I recommend them that, in all cases, when allowed, they
labor faithfully for reasonable wages.

"And I further declare and make known, that

such persons, of suitable condition, will be received into the armed service of the United States, to garrison forts, positions, stations, and other places, and to man vessels of all sorts in said service.

"And upon this act, sincerely believed to be an act of justice, warranted by the Constitution upon military necessity, I invoke the considerate judgment of mankind and the gracious favor of Almighty God."

Thenceforward the freedmen and the colored men of the free States were received freely into the service, uniformed in the garb of American soldiers; and to the two hundred thousand who thus bravely came to the country's rescue, and bravely fought beneath her banners, the future historian will award the honor of having turned the scale of battle in favor of liberty, and thus having secured the perpetuity of free institutions on this continent.

In his annual message, delivered December 1, 1862, between the issuing of the preliminary and final Proclamations of Emancipation, he defended his course in the following language:

"The dogmas of the quiet past are inadequate to the stormy present. The occasion is piled high with difficulty, and we must rise with the occasion. As our case is new, so we must think anew and act anew. We must disenthrall ourselves, and then we shall save our country.

"Fellow-citizens, *we* can not escape history. We of this Congress and this Administration will be remembered in spite of ourselves. No personal significance or insignificance can spare one or another of us. The fiery trial through which we pass will light us down in honor or dishonor to the latest generation. * * In giving freedom to the *slave* we assure freedom to the *free*—honorable alike to what we give and what we preserve. We shall nobly save or meanly lose the last hope of earth. Other means *may* succeed—*this can not fail.* The way is plain, peaceful, generous, just—a way which, if pursued, the world will forever applaud and God forever bless."

Mr. Lincoln viewed the calamities of the nation from the stand-point of a Christian as well as that of a statesman. In his last inaugural he said:

"It may seem strange that any men should dare to ask God's assistance in wringing their bread from the sweat of other men's faces; but

let us judge not, that we be not judged. * *
The Almighty has his own purposes. 'Woe
unto the world because of offenses, for it must
needs be that offenses come; but woe unto that
man by whom the offenses cometh.' If we shall
suppose American slavery is one of those offenses
which, in the providence of God, must needs
come, but which, having continued through his
appointed time, he now wills to remove, and
that he gives to both North and South this terrible war as the woe due to those by whom the
offense came, shall we discern therein any departure from those divine attributes which the
believers in a living God always ascribe to him?
Fondly do we hope, fervently do we pray, that
this mighty scourge of war may speedily pass
away. Yet if God wills that it continue until
all the wealth piled by the bondman's two hundred and fifty years of unrequited toil shall be
sunk, and until every drop of blood drawn with
the lash shall be paid with another drawn with
the sword, as was said three thousand years ago,
so still it must be said, 'The judgments of the
Lord are true and righteous altogether.'"

Another incident highly characteristic of Mr.
Lincoln was brought about by the banishment

of a rebel sympathizer of Ohio into the rebel lines, after trial and conviction by court-martial. A committee of gentlemen, members of Congress and prominent politicians from Ohio, whose sympathies were against the war, called upon Mr. Lincoln with a paper, which they read to him, arguing against the legality or justice of this act of banishment. Lincoln replied in writing, discussing the points presented with much minuteness, particularity, and cogency of reasoning. Well knowing that this would be lost equally upon them and upon the political party which they represented, he resorted to an appeal which not only set the whole question at rest, but also placed his opponents in a most embarrassing dilemma:

"I send you," he wrote, "duplicates of this letter, in order that you, or a majority of you, may, if you choose, indorse your names upon them, and return them thus indorsed to me, with the understanding that those signing are thereby committed to the following propositions:

"1. That there is now a rebellion in the United States, the object and tendency of which is to destroy the National Union, and that, in your opinion, an army and navy are constitutional means for suppressing that rebellion.

"2. That no one of you will do any thing which, in his own judgment, will tend to hinder the increase, or favor the decrease, or lessen the efficiency of the army and navy, while engaged in the effort to suppress that rebellion; and,

"3. That each of you will, in his sphere, do all he can to have the officers, and soldiers, and seamen of the army and navy, while engaged in the effort to suppress the rebellion, paid, fed, clad, and otherwise well provided and supported.

"And with the further understanding that, upon receiving this letter, with the names thus indorsed, I will cause them to be published, which publication shall be, within itself, a revocation of the order in relation to Mr. Vallandigham."

It may seem strange that to men making any pretensions whatever to patriotism—to men not avowedly enemies of their country and in league with the rebels—propositions like the above could involve any questionable alternative; and yet had they indorsed these propositions, they would have condemned their own partisan principles. If they refused, they made it obvious to all men that not only the banished convict, but they themselves were disloyal men. They preferred the latter horn of the dilemma, refused to indorse the propositions, and left their *confrere* under the military sentence of banishment to rebeldom.

The battle of Gettysburg, on the first three days of July, 1863, is regarded as approaching nearer to the honor of a "decisive battle" than any other of the war. Thenceforward the rebellion steadily retrograded till it was crushed out. The victory was hung in the balance, and was only won by the most stubborn and heroic efforts on the part of the Union forces. Had it gone against them, our country would have been in a different position from that which she now occupies. The people, grateful to the thousands of brave and patriotic dead who fell there, purchased the field for a national cemetery. Mr. Lincoln was invited to attend the ceremonies of dedication. He there delivered the following brief address :

" Four-score and seven years ago our fathers brought forth upon this continent a new nation, conceived in liberty and dedicated to the proposition that all men are created equal. Now we are engaged in a great civil war, testing whether that nation, or any nation so conceived and so dedicated, can long endure. We are met on the great battle-field of that war. We are met to dedicate a portion of it as the final resting-place of those who here gave their lives that the nation might live. It is altogether fitting and proper that we should do this.

"But in a larger sense, we can not dedicate, we can not consecrate this ground. The brave men, living and dead, who struggled here, have consecrated it far above our power to add or detract. The world will little note nor long remember what we say here, but it can never forget what they did here. It is for us, the living, rather to be dedicated here to the unfinished work that they have thus far so nobly carried on. It is rather for us to be here dedicated to the great task remaining before us; that from these honored dead we take increased devotion to the cause for which they here gave the last full measure of devotion; that we here highly resolve that the dead shall not have died in vain; that the nation shall, under God, have a new birth to freedom, and that the Government of the people, by the people, and for the people, shall not perish from the earth."

That "the world will little note nor long remember" what Lincoln said there, was a mistaken prophecy. It will be read and admired so long as Gettysburg is remembered as a battlefield of freedom.

The Union National Convention which met in Baltimore in June, 1864, nominated Mr. Lincoln for reëlection without a dissenting voice; and yet such was the *apparent* national discontent with the management of affairs, and such the apparent weariness and impatience of the people under the crushing burdens of the war, that the success of the Unionists at the election was for a time regarded as very doubtful. The opposition were clamorous for compromise, concession to the rebels, abrogation of the Proclamation of Emancipation—in short, for " peace at *any* price:" and the noisiness of these time-servers made them appear to be much more numerous and formidable than they really were. To foster this spirit and to furnish them electioneering capital, the rebel government sent emissaries to Canada, who announced themselves peace commissioners, authorized to propose terms for the cessation of hostilities. Lincoln declined to hold any official intercourse with them, but published the following proclamation

"EXECUTIVE MANSION, ⎫
"WASHINGTON, July 8, 1864. ⎭

"TO WHOM IT MAY CONCERN:

"Any proposition which embraces the restoration of peace, the integrity of the whole Union, *and the abandonment of slavery*, and which comes by and with an authority that can control the armies now at war against the United States, will be received and considered by the Executive Government of the United States, and will be met by liberal terms on other substantial and collateral points, and the bearer or bearers thereof shall have safe conduct both ways.

"ABRAHAM LINCOLN."

This was regarded by many of the Union party to be a great political blunder, and one which might result in the triumph of the " peace-at-any-price party," and in that view greatly to be deplored. Lincoln's reply was that, " If I go down, I will go down, like the Cumberland, with my colors flying." He meant to stand by justice and principle, sink or swim, and he did it.

Another great "blunder" was perpetrated by the President-candidate soon after. Sherman was beating Johnson back step by step upon Atlanta, and Grant fixing his grip firmly upon Richmond, but the terms of enlistment of many

thousands of soldiers were expiring, the waste
of war was thinning our ranks, and it became
necessary to the continued success of the armies
for the President to repeat his call, so often before sounded over the land, for "five hundred
thousand more." His over-cautious political
friends protested that it would be suicide to lay
this new burden on the people on the eve of the
Presidential election. It was urged that Grant
and Sherman could at least hold their own during the brief time to elapse previous to the
election, and that if the election was lost the
cause would be lost. Mr. Lincoln replied that
his duty required him to sustain the armies who
were fighting at the front; that the election was
no part of his business—the people must attend
to that; and, at any rate, he had perfect confidence in the patriotism of the masses and the
favor of God. The wheels of the lot again
began revolving in every provost-marshal's district, and the song of July, 1862, was again
heard :

" We are coming, Father Abraham, five hundred thou-
sand more;
From Mississippi's winding stream, and from New
England's shore;

We leave our plows and workshops, our wives and
    children dear,
With hearts too full for utterance, with but a silent tear:
We dare not look behind us, but steadfastly before;
We are coming, Father Abraham, five hundred thou-
    sand more!"

The Five Hundred Thousand came forth, and
Abraham Lincoln was reëlected, while the columns were marching in, by the heaviest majorities ever rolled up for a presidential candidate.

Then Sherman marched to the sea, and up
through the hot-bed of secession, South Carolina, leaving ruin in his track, and sending
despair to traitorous hearts. Grant dealt his un-
ceasing and tremendous blows upon the stag-
gering rebellion at Richmond. The crash came
sudden and resounding as the fall of some mon-
arch tree in the forest, and the long, glad shout
of triumph rang and reëchoed from Maine to
California.

As the last battles at Richmond drew near,
Mr. Lincoln went to City Point, to be near the
field of operations and convenient for any emergency in which his presence would be desirable.
When the news came of the evacuation of Richmond by the feeble remnant of the late power-

ful rebel army, he took a steamer, and, in company with Admiral Porter, and his little son, whom he held by the hand, steamed up the river, and was landed with a small boat in the rebel city. An eye-witness, Mr. C. C. Coffin, thus describes the scene: "He entered the city unheralded; six sailors armed with carbines stepped upon the shore, followed by the President, his son, and Admiral Porter; the officers followed, and six marines brought up the rear.

"There were thirty or forty freedmen who had been sole possessors of themselves for twenty-four hours, at work on the bank of the canal. Somehow they obtained the information that the man who was head and shoulders taller than all others around him, with features large and irregular, with a mild eye and a pleasant countenance, was President Lincoln.

"'God bless you, sah!' said one, taking off his cap and bowing very low.

"'Hurrah! hurrah! President Linkum has come!' rang through the streets.

"The lieutenant found himself without a command. What cared these freedmen, fresh from the house of bondage, for military orders! Their deliverer had come—he who, next to the Lord

Jesus, was their best friend. It was not a hurrah they gave, but a wild jubilant cry of inexpressible joy. They gathered around the President, ran ahead, hovered upon the flanks of the little company, and hung like a dark cloud upon the rear. Men, women, and children joined the constantly-increasing throng; they came from all the by-streets, running in breathless haste, shouting, hallooing, and dancing with delight. The men threw up their hats, the women waved their bonnets and handkerchiefs, clapped their hands, and sang, 'Glory to God! glory! glory! glory!' rendering all the praise to God, who had heard their wailings in the past, their moanings for wives, husbands, children, and friends sold out of their sight, had given them freedom, and, after long years of waiting, had permitted them thus unexpectedly to behold the face of their great benefactor.

"'I thank you, dear Jesus, that I behold President Linkum,' was the exclamation of a woman who stood upon the threshold of her humble home, and, with streaming eyes and clasped hands, gave thanks aloud to the Savior of men. Another, more demonstrative in her joy, was jumping and striking her hands with

all her might, crying, 'Bless de Lord! bless
de Lord!' as if there could be no end of her
thanksgiving. The air rang with a tumultuous
chorus of voices. The street became almost
impassable on account of the increasing multitude. Soldiers were summoned to clear the
way. How strange the event! The President
of the United States—he who had been hated
and maligned above all other men living, to
whom the vilest epithets had been applied by
the people of Richmond—was walking their
streets, receiving the thanksgivings, blessings,
and praises from thousands of those who received
him as the ally of the Messiah!"

The walk was long and the way obstructed
by the blackened ruins of the part of the city
swept by a devastating conflagration a short
time previous, as well as by the throngs of jubilant freedmen. Pausing to rest a moment, an
aged negro removed his tattered hat from his
fleecy locks, and, with a deep obeisance, said:
"May de good Lord bless you, President Linkum!" The President reverently removed his
own hat and bowed to the man, representative
of his race, who had for three-score years borne
the blows and insults of the cruel oppressor.

11

He was the first public man who, during these long years of the reign of injustice, had recognized, in a slave State, the manhood of the bondman. In God's good providence their haughty oppressors will erelong be compelled, both as individuals and as States, to do the same.

Mr. Lincoln remained in Richmond two days, rode through the streets, visited the prisons and fortifications, ordered bread to be distributed to the famished rebel families left behind, and to the freed people, and then took his departure for home.

He witnessed scenes of the most profound significance. The blackened city, the ashes of that resplendent castle in the air, the Southern Empire, the broken fetters of slavery, and heard that shout of deliverance of millions of slaves, which once to hear was worth a lifetime of labor and toil. He stood there, as Moses stood upon Mount Nebo, and gazed from the departing mists upon a bright and far-reaching future, prosperous in the reign of peace, justice, and freedom. A glad day was this for Mr. Lincoln, a memorable day in the annals of the irrepressible and ever-recurring conflicts in defense of the rights of man.

O, land, through years of shrouded nights
  In triple blackness groping,
Toward the far-prophetic lights
  That beacon the world's hoping,
Behold, no tittle thou shalt miss
  Of that transforming given
To all who, dragged through hell's abyss,
  Hold fast their grip on heaven.

The Lord God's purpose throbs along
  Our stormy turbulances;
He keeps the sap of nations strong
  By hidden recompenses.
The Lord God sows his righteous grain
  In battle-blasted furrows,
And draws from present days of pain
  Large peace for calm to-morrows.

  *   *   *   *   *

For lo! the branding flails that drave
  Our husks of foul self from us,
Show all the watching heavens we have
  Immortal grains of promise.
And lo! the dreadful blasts that blew
  In gusts of fire amid us,
Have scorched and winnowed from the true
  The falseness which undid us.

Wherefore, O ransomed people shout!
  O, banners, wave in glory!
O, bugles, blow the triumph out!

O, drums, strike up the story!
Clang, broken fetters, idle swords!
Clap hands, O States, together!
AND LET ALL PRAISES BE THE LORD'S,
OUR SAVIOR AND OUR FATHER!

Lieut. RICHARD REALF.

CHAPTER XVII.

RETURN TO WASHINGTON—DEATH AND BURIAL.

R. LINCOLN remained in Richmond two days, looking over the great fortifications of that rebel stronghold, and gathering such information as might be of value in his future duties.

On his return, he stopped at City Point. "Calling upon the head surgeon at that place, Mr. Lincoln told him that he wished to visit all the hospitals under his charge, and shake hands with every soldier. The surgeon asked if he knew what he was undertaking, there being five or six thousand soldiers at that place, and it would be quite a task upon his strength to visit all the wards and shake hands with every soldier. Mr. Lincoln answered, with a smile, he 'guessed he was equal to the task; at any rate he would try, and go as far as he could.

He should never probably see the boys again, and he wanted them to know that he appreciated what they had done for their country.' Finding it useless to dissuade him, the surgeon began his rounds with the President, who walked from bed to bed, extending his hand to all, saying a few words of sympathy to some, making kind inquiries of others, and welcomed by all with the heartiest cordiality. As they passed along, they came to a ward in which lay a rebel who had been wounded and was a prisoner. As the tall figure of the kindly visitor appeared in sight, he was recognized by the rebel soldier, who, raising himself on his elbow in bed, watched Mr. Lincoln as he approached, and, extending his hand, exclaimed, while tears ran down his cheeks: 'Mr. Lincoln, I have long wanted to see you, to ask your forgiveness for ever raising my hand against the old flag.' Mr. Lincoln was moved to tears. He heartily shook the hand of the repentant rebel, and assured him of his good-will, and, with a few words of kind advice, passed on. After some hours, the tour of the various hospitals was made, and Mr. Lincoln returned with the surgeon to his office. They had scarcely entered, however, when a messenger came, saying that one ward had been omitted, and 'the boys wanted to see the President.' The surgeon, who was thoroughly tired, and knew Mr. Lincoln must be, tried to dissuade him from going, but the good man said he must go back; he 'would not knowingly omit one, the boys would be so disappointed.' So he went with the messenger, accompanied by the surgeon, and shook hands with the gratified soldiers, and then returned again to the office. The surgeon expressed the fear that the President's arm would be lamed with so much hand-shaking, saying that it certainly must ache. Mr. Lincoln smiled, and, saying something about his strong muscles, stepped out at the open door, took up a very large, heavy ax which lay there, by a log of wood, and chopped vigorously for a few moments, sending the chips flying in all directions; and then pausing, he extended his right arm to its full length, holding the ax out horizontally without its even quivering as he held it. Strong men who looked on, men accustomed to manual labor, could not hold the ax in that position for a moment. Returning to the office, he took a glass of lemonade—for he would take no stronger beverage—and while he was in, the chips he had chopped were gathered up and safely cared for by a hospital steward, because they were the chips that 'Father Abraham' chopped."

He returned to Washington on that ever-memorable Tenth of April when the whole land was resplendent with banners and the air vibrating with the music of bands. No sooner had he received the embraces of his family, than his residence was surrounded by thousands of people, determined to see him and compel him to speak. He appeared and made a little speech, which he said he thought would be sufficient to "disperse them," but they would not be "dispersed." Appearing at a later hour, he said:

" I am greatly rejoiced that an occasion has occurred so pleasurable that the people can't restrain themselves. I suppose that arrangements are being made for some sort of formal demonstration. If there should be such a demonstration, I, of course, shall have to respond to it, and I shall have nothing to say if I dribble it out before. [Laughter, and cries of 'We want to hear you now.'] I see you have a band. [Voice, 'We have three of them.'] I propose now closing up by requesting you to play a certain air or tune. I have always thought 'Dixie' one of the best tunes I ever heard. [Laughter.] I have heard that our adversaries over the way have attempted to appropriate it as a national air. I insisted, yesterday, that we had fairly captured it. I presented this question to the Attorney-General, and he gave his opinion that it is our lawful prize. [Laughter and cheers.] I ask the band to give us a good turn upon it."

The tune was played vigorously, and Mr. Lincoln retired. On the 11th of April he issued a proclamation requiring foreign nations to accord to our war vessels all the privileges and immunities of a friendly power at peace, on the penalty, should they refuse, of placing the same restrictions upon their vessels that they did upon ours.

This was his last official act. On the 14th he went out to ride with Mrs. Lincoln, and was in an unusually happy mood. He spoke to her hopefully of rest from his years of exhaustive care and toil, and of a visit to their old home. From his inauguration onward he frequently received letters threatening his life, and often expressed a presentiment that he would not long survive. But the sunlight of peace which broke upon the country had driven those gloomy forebodings away from his heart, and he was full of happiness, and full of generous and benevolent emotions toward his late enemies and antagonists.

At the suggestion of some friends, it was arranged, during the day, that General Grant and the President should attend a play at Ford's Theater in the evening. To this Mr. Lincoln consented, and about nine o'clock, in company with Mrs. Lincoln, entered the theater, taking a private box above the stage. General Grant was called away by business and left the city early in the evening. While the play was progressing. Mr. Lincoln seemed amused by the entertainment, and smiled and conversed in a lively mood to those near him. Suddenly a pistol-shot resounded through the house, and a man leaped from Mr. Lincoln's box upon the stage, brandished a knife in a tragical manner, and disappeared behind the scenes. The screams of Mrs. Lincoln, an instant later, revealed what had taken place, and the audience sprang to their feet in wildest excitement and horror. One of the audience pursued the assassin, and saw him mount and ride swiftly away. Mr. Lincoln had fallen slightly forward and was insensible. The shot had taken effect in the back part of the head, and was at once known to be mortal. He was carried to a house opposite, and surgeons and friends gathered around. During the night, he breathed at times easily, and at other times so laboriously that the friends who were present gathered around to see the last. At six o'clock in the morning his struggle was over, and his spirit took its flight from the earth.

At the same hour in which the fatal shot was fired in Ford's Theater, an assassin forced his way into the sick chamber where Mr. Seward, Secretary of State, was lying prostrate with disease, and stabbed him repeatedly, striking down and killing one attendant who came to his rescue, and severely wounding others. Mr. Seward, after receiving the first blow, sought escape by rolling off the back part of the bed, and, though severely injured, recovered both from his disease and the wounds inflicted by the assassin.

The assassin of Mr. Lincoln was recognized, as he crossed the stage after committing the deed, as a play-actor named Wilkes Booth; and, although for a few days he eluded pursuit, he was traced up, surrounded in a barn, where he had taken refuge, and was shot in the head by a soldier and killed. His body was cast— none but two men intrusted with the task know where. The assassin who attempted the life of Mr. Seward and the immediate accomplices of Booth were captured, tried, and hung.

On the 14th of April the country was in the height of its joy over the glorious termination of four long years of dreadful war. On the morning of the 15th the terrible news of the assassination flew to the remotest villages, and the nation stood overwhelmed with horror and grief. The sun-and-storm-beaten soldier, the aged patriot on his staff, the strong man in his prime, bent like rushes and wept and sobbed like children. The death of no other man since time began carried sorrow to so many hearts and drew tears from so many eyes as the tragic death of Abraham Lincoln. Most appalling it was to the poor colored people. They had looked to him as their deliverer, their tender father, their protector, almost their earthly all. In some of their simple hearts he was enshrined and endowed with superhuman attributes. They

regarded him as clothed with wisdom and love,
in some degree approaching and resembling the
attributes of JESUS. He fell beneath the malice
of that system which had so long and so terribly
trampled them to the earth, and they could only
find comfort in casting themselves upon the
mighty arm of their Father, God.

The body of the dead emancipator was em-
balmed and borne on its funeral march to his
home in Springfield. No such funeral proces-
sion has the world ever seen—probably will never
see again. The cities and villages radiant, but
a brief time before, with banners and illumina-
tions were hung, street by street, with heavy
folds of black drapery. Tens of thousands
pressed to cast a last sad gaze at that cold face,
and sobbed aloud at the mournful view. Arriving at Springfield, he was entombed in a family
vault; and thus, glorious in life and grand in
death, passed away the great and good President.

The death-shot under which the President fell
was such as to extinguish sensation and conscious-
ness instantly. He did not, could not know, while
his spirit lingered in the body, any thing of what
had been done. The pall of darkness and insensi-

bility fell upon him in the twinkling of an eye; he, therefore, suffered no pain. Other martyrs have passed through the fire and the torments invented by human malignity—have had to nerve themselves for days and weeks in anticipation of the ordeal through which they were called to pass. Lincoln was suddenly called from the triumph on earth, as we may fondly trust, to the triumph in salvation through the merits of Jesus, without a conscious struggle or a pang of mind or of body.

In extreme contrast with the last days and death of the illustrious victim was the close of the career of the assassin. Vengeance leaped upon him while the report of his murderous pistol-shot yet echoed through the hall—not with sudden annihilation, but with the first pang of protracted torment. Springing down from the box to the stage of the theater, his leg was broken near the ankle by the fall; and although he succeeded in reaching and mounting his horse, the rugged bones of his broken limb lacerated the flesh at every leap of his flight. Having secreted himself in a swamp, the agony of his swollen leg · was lost in the fiercer pangs of despair. Abhorred and hunted down with implacable animosity, he wrote in his diary that God could not pardon a crime which proved so revolting to human nature. Detested, abandoned, starving, in agony and weakness of body, and in despair, listening with alert terror for the footsteps of the avenger, not a word of sympathy or cheer, not an act of kindness, with no possible relief except through death, and no exit from death but into hell—so he passed the few days between his crime and his painful, bloody end.

While we can not, in most instances, safely ascribe overwhelming disaster to the retributive justice of God, yet that the Almighty does, on some occasions, suddenly follow crime with terrible evidences of his indignation is beyond peradventure. So marked have been the examples of instant vengeance on atrocious crimes, that in every age and every land the fact has been impressed on the human mind. His "burning coals of juniper" and his "sharp arrows" flash and fly even in a world designed to be probationary. The persistency with which horrible disease, horrible death, and intolerable anguish of soul have pursued the Herods, Neros, and such like monsters of iniquity, is a fact too sharply defined to admit of cavil. And yet amid all such instances there is none more clearly marked than the instant torment which, without human agency, followed the crime of the assassination.

CHAPTER XVIII.

LESSONS FROM THE LIFE OF ABRAHAM LINCOLN.

I. THE SECRET OF HIS SUCCESS.

THE Presidency of the United States is an exalted position, but it proved only a subordinate accessory to the fame of Abraham Lincoln. We have had many Presidents, of whom some were only lifted sufficiently high by their official honors to be within the reach of the scorn and contempt of good men. But Lincoln's name and fame is forever linked with that of Washington, on a level of equal elevation. No names in the history of any land stand above them, none so universally command the admiration of mankind. England has her Hampden and Cromwell, Russia her Peter the Great, Germany her Charles V and Frederick, Sweden her Gustavus Adolphus; France can only point to Charles Martel and Henry IV,

12

despots of surpassing ability, and conquerors of
terrible power.   Among these, none but Hampden and Cromwell can be considered as approaching comparison with the two most honored
names of America, and these awaken but qualified
admiration, and that with few others than Eng-
lishmen or their descendants, while the "Father"
and the "Preserver" of America are subjects of
enthusiastic eulogy in every civilized nation.

The qualifications of mind and heart which
raised this man of humble origin, lowly life, and
self-distrust to this great elevation should be
deeply pondered by every young man.   They
were—

1. HONESTY.   His success in life, from the
first, was mainly the result of this trait in his
character.   He would have failed in every department of life without it.   As a laborer, a flat-
boatman, clerk, surveyor, legislator, lawyer, and
as President, the secret of his power was the un-
qualified confidence his employers and the people had in his incorruptible, unswerving integrity.
Every one who knew him knew they could de-
pend upon him in every undertaking, from the
smallest pecuniary transaction to the emancipation of a race.   *Failure* was possible in all these;

but in calculating the probabilities of success, it was in no case necessary to make any allowance for possible insincerity or evasion on the part of Abraham Lincoln. He had superiors in eloquence and intellectual gifts, and few prominent men who were not superior to him in general education and acquirements. With a fair share of all these, and excelling in the one great element of his success, he rose immeasurably above them. It is to be observed that this was not honesty in its limited sense, as applied to truth and rectitude in business relations, but in its broader sense of justice, respect for the *rights* of all men, pecuniary, civil, and political. While honesty made him President, it dictated his immortal Proclamation of Emancipation, and rendered him the unfaltering champion of the liberty and equality of all men.

2. HUMILITY. In the highest reach of his fame, in the hours of most brilliant success, in his broadest grasp of power, not a trace of pride or arrogance was seen in his simple and transparent nature. His elevation he attributed to the too partial estimate of the people. His successes he referred, at once and always, to "the gracious favor of Almighty God."

This unaffected humility, while gathering honors and achieving triumphs which would have lifted other men's heads high in self-confidence and pride, enkindled a love in the hearts of the people for him of which they then knew little till it burst forth in irrepressible grief at his loss. It is a remarkable commentary on human perverseness, that while millions cherish the memory of an imperfect man with affection, for benefactions rendered with modesty, the larger part of them regard without emotion the infinitely sweeter and more profound humility and benevolence of our Lord and Savior Jesus Christ.

3. " CHARITY suffereth long and is kind ; charity envieth not; charity vaunteth not itself, is not puffed up ; * * is not easily provoked; thinketh no evil." It is not too much to say that this beautiful language may be used with little qualification in describing the mind and heart of Abraham Lincoln. That such attractive Christian virtues are not more frequently recognized and rewarded by the people, is only because they are not exhibited by the men of intellect who aspire to public favor.

4. INDUSTRY and PERSEVERANCE. From childhood till death, Abraham Lincoln was a willing,

cheerful, hopeful son of toil. No labor was
avoided because of its severity. The idea probably never occurred to him that any kind of
hard labor in the fields, woods, on the river, or
mental drudgery in his profession was too hard
or not sufficiently dignified for him. His rough,
horny hands, badges of humble labor, were not
to him either suggestive of disgrace or of pride.
Met by disheartening discouragements, he struggled hopefully against hope, persevered against
the greatest obstacles, and, whether elated or
depressed in spirits, *worked on.* So great was
his mental and physical exhaustion, at the time
of the battle of Chicamauga, that he said:
"Would to God I could rest in death on the
field with those brave boys!" Exhausted, dis-
spirited, apparently discouraged, he *toiled on*
till that last, dreamless sleep fell upon him.

5. FAITH IN GOD. "Ask and ye shall receive."
He believed that God would give him wisdom,
guide him by his counsels, and maintain the
cause of justice and truth. It was doubtless
this confidence that lifted him above unjust ex-
pedients, and gave him that fearless adherence
to principle which marked his whole life. He
was confident that the great struggle for free-

dom and justice was embraced in God's plans, would be shaped by his purposes; that he was only a humble instrument whose business it was to execute God's will. Without this faith, he would have hesitated oftentimes and faltered, but to falter was to fail and bring ruin and disaster upon the cause of his country.

Honesty, humility, industry, benevolence, and trust in God's providence—such were elements in the character which God, in his love and mercy, placed at the head of our nation in its trying hour. To him be the praise.

II. THE THEATER.

Mr. Lincoln's usefulness and his fame were almost wholly due to the practice of those principles and the exhibition of those traits which lead us to trust that he was a true Christian; yet he met his death in the box of a theater, a circumstance which was not only deeply humiliating and painful to those who loved and honored him most, but one which, by the force of example, is fraught with irreparable evil. As time passes away, and the faults and follies which are inseparable from human character fall from his name into forgetfulness, this fact, stead-

fast as his fame, will be read and remembered.
And yet this circumstance can scarcely be plead
in honor of those houses of iniquity. The fact
that the stage was selected for the scene of the
foulest deed in the annals of crime, that the
perpetrator was one of the most popular in the
theatrical profession, and that his immediate
accomplices were habitues of such places, are
surely not facts to which any advocate of thea-
ters can refer with complaisance.

- The Christian will remember that, if Mr. Lincoln had boldly taken position with Christ's dis-
ciples, and consistently adhered to the precepts
of the Gospel, he would not have died in the
theater, and might not have fallen at all at the
hand of an assassin.

We may charitably suppose that Mr. Lincoln
visited the theater as a momentary relaxation
of his overtaxed mind, as an opportunity to
cast aside his cares and relieve himself from his
anxieties. Why may not others do the same
and remain innocent? What evil is there in
the gaslight, music, and pantomime of the stage?
Let us answer these questions briefly:

1. The playwrights who construct the fictions
now displayed upon the stage are, without a sol-

itary exception, enemies of our Lord and Savior, and hence at heart scoffers at piety; most of them have been open and profane revilers of pure religion; many of them grossly immoral, sensual, and debauched. These traits exhibited in their lives permeate their productions, and are hidden, in part only, by a tawdry veil of mock morality. Are such writers fit instructors of those who wish to attain purity of mind and life?

2. The play-actors, men and women—who and what are they? It is sufficient to answer that the very names "actor" and "actress" have become the synonyms of immorality and vice. There are, it is true, exceptions. There are even those in whom a solitary virtue shines out with peculiar brightness, but *these are exceptions.* The rule is, that not only the moralities but the decencies of life are ignored and disregarded. Are *such* persons such as those who would avoid the misery and ruin of vicious courses should sit beneath and listen to?

3. The surroundings of the theater—what are they? Not a house of that kind in the world but casts its shadow and sustains by its influence a drinking saloon, a gambling den, and, more or less directly, other places not fit to be

named. Why are these avenues to destruction and death crowded, with open portals, close around the theater? Because the entrance into the theater is the first step into their jaws. If fascinated by the false lights into the first, the steps are easily and almost certainly taken, by short gradations, into the others.

4. The pretense that the rewards of virtue and punishments of vice are exhibited there, is a sham as obvious as their tawdry costumes. No reasonable mind would pretend that such characters, in such a place, would seek to promote purity among the people. Their *success* in obtaining money is dependent upon, and inseparable from, their success in depraving and polluting the minds of their auditors.

5. The pleasure they offer by their displays is not worthy the name. The fact that it sickens and palls so quickly on the senses of even those who have succeeded in drowning their conscientious scruples against such exhibitions, is one reason why the deeper excitement of the saloon and the gaming-table is so quickly sought by its devotees.

6. The audience of the stage—of whom is it composed? Not a thief, robber, gambler, bur-

glar, or harlot can be found, in any city, who does not make the theater a place of regular resort. Without the patronage of the classes of most grossly immoral people, not one-fourth of these institutions could be sustained. The performances are, and must of necessity be, adapted to their tastes and preferences. Many respectable and moral people are found associated with them in witnessing the same exhibitions; but is such the company in which those who desire to honor God and win everlasting life would desire their Lord and Master to find them? Is it possible to plunge in such a pool without contamination?

But from this sad chapter, this humiliating circumstance, let us turn away.

III. THE PROVIDENCE OF GOD.

In no chapter of the history of man was the sovereignty of God more clearly manifest than in the American civil war. It stood out so obvious as to attract the attention of the most stolid and unbelieving. As each inexplicable event, disaster, and defeat burst upon the country, the question seemed to rise involuntarily on every hand, "What are God's designs in this?"

Many of these purposes very soon were unveiled. We all have seen the necessity of the defeat of the Union army at Bull Run, and other reverses in the early part of the conflict, and know that without them no lasting peace could have been attained. This subject opens a wide and fruitful field for most interesting investigation, which will doubtless hereafter be traversed by some one capable of the task. Let us notice a few evidences of God's providence:

1. All Christian men of thought and intelligence knew that God would destroy slavery. For seventy years this prophecy was reiterated in every part of the Christian world. *How* he would do it none could tell. When that institution had attained the very summit of its insolent pride and its triumphant influence, and seemed intrenched in impregnable power, *it suddenly fell.*

2. When God had prepared his instrument, and was moving him forward to do his work, how poor and inadequate that instrument appeared! Rebeldom laughed aloud in derision. "Ape," "idiot," "buffoon," "imbecile," were epithets that came from every rebel chief, as the sad, self-distrustful embassador of God's

justice advanced to the seat of Government.
The wise heads of Europe were shaken in utter
distrust of the "ignorant backwoods attorney."
Patriotic hearts failed as their anxious eyes
detected supposed evidences of vascillation and
fear. As time progressed and events crowded
fast, conviction and surprise took the place of distrust, and the London Times exclaimed, "That
ignorant pilot may yet blunder into port."
There was no blundering about it; God makes
no mistakes.

3. The work of deliverance was long in preparation. While the slave-mother was bewailing
her stolen offspring, while the whip whistled in
its swift descent upon the quivering back, while
the coffle plodded its sorrowful way, the energies for reprieve and retribution were gathering
strength.

A tough, elastic physical constitution was required for the emancipator; a weakling would
have failed. It was prepared in the Western
clearing, and tested by wrestling with the trees
of the forest. Prudence and caution were requisite; inconsiderate or passionate rashness would
have ruined the cause. High moral qualities
were indispensable—incorruptible integrity, per-

severance, hopefulness, intense hatred of injustice, and delicate regard for human rights, humility, moral courage, and endurance—inflexible firmness for principle—and, as a sheet-anchor, childlike confidence in God.

These were furnished forth from a backwoods cabin, molded by an unknown and illiterate Christian mother, disciplined by the hardships and vicissitudes of toilsome pioneer life, led by gradual steps of promotion into power, and brought into requisition at the exact time when needed.

Mr. Lincoln's first nomination for the Presidency was seemingly the result of accident, and against the probabilities as understood by his supporters. This and all the other events of his rise and progress in life, when viewed in the light of God's purpose to destroy slavery, exhibit *design*, and the most exact adaptation of the means to the end in view. The preparation of the work is equally obvious to us now. The aggressions of the slave power, the defeat of the antislavery candidate four years before, when his success would have precipitated the conflict before either the people or the leader were prepared for the work—even the bountiful harvests poured upon us during the great struggle, when our barns and store-houses were crowded to overflowing with the lavish gifts of God's providence.

The combination of the "blunders" and "accidents" of the war, in the establishment of union, liberty, and justice, is referred to by the New York *Herald* as something strange and inexplicable in history. In an issue in March, 1867, that irreligious paper says:

"It is curious to note how the accidents of the war and the blunders of opposing politicians have assisted in the work of this great political revolution. A decisive defeat of the rebels at the first Bull Run fight might have saved Southern slavery in the collapse of the Jeff. Davis confederacy. Had McClellan succeeded at Richmond, there would most likely have been no Emancipation Proclamation from President Lincoln. Had Andrew Johnson, when called to take his place, convened Congress for the legislative work of Southern reconstruction instead of undertaking it himself, the States concerned would doubtless have been restored upon a half-way compromise on negro suffrage. Had those States followed the example of Tennessee, they would now be in Congress on the same terms. Had the Democrats in the House voted for this last bill as it came from the Senate, they would have secured to the leading rebels the privilege, now denied them, of assisting in rebuilding their respective States. As our failures in the war in defense of slavery brought about the extirpation of slavery, so all our failures in half-way plans of restoration have worked out a full and decisive settlement on the basis of civil and political equality."

" Surely the wrath of man shall praise thee." The demonstration of God's providence afforded by the facts of our history are a source of great joy and encouragement to every Christian patriot. We may labor on in the cause of liberty and human brotherhood—in the whole cause of Christ, with the perfect assurance that the very machinations and inventions of the devil and of oppressors will be made by the great Ruler to work with and for us. With such evidences of God's aid, despondency is sin, discouragement is doubt of God's faithfulness.

CHAPTER XIX.

TRIBUTES TO HIS CHARACTER FROM EUROPE.

THERE was no circumstance attending the bereavement of the American people so grateful to them, in their grief, as the expressions of sympathy and appreciation which came from Europe. The avowed and active hostility of the ruling classes in England and France; the words of reproach and ridicule which came by every steamer during the continuance of the war, and the aid they rendered to the rebels had aroused the resentment of the nation to an extent that rendered a war of retaliation on our part a probable event. This animosity was drowned in tears over Lincoln's grave. The London *Times*, the busy and able detractor of our country, said:

" The news will be received in this country with sorrow as sincere and profound as it awoke even in the United States."

This proved to be true. The sensation produced throughout the kingdom was intense, and pervaded all classes from the throne to the hovel. The Queen, without delay, sent a letter of condolence to the bereaved family. Both houses of Parliament, meeting, passed resolutions of sympathy with the American people. A nobleman who had favored the rebel cause said: " Nothing but the death of our own Queen could have produced such sincere sorrow in the breast of every Englishman." Public meetings were held, business suspended, buildings draped in black, and every indication of public grief manifested in all parts of the country. The effect was similar, though perhaps to a less extent, in Germany, Russia, Italy, and France. Even the Sultan of Turkey, separated so far from us by space, ideas, and religion, sent his words of condolence and sympathy.

The London *News* said:

" In all time to come, among all who think of manhood more than rank, the name of Lincoln will be held in reverence."

The London *Telegraph* said :

" From corruption, hatred, jealousy, or uncharitableness this great ruler was wholly free."

13

The London *Globe* said:

"The news from America will send a thrill of horror throughout the land. It is too soon to estimate the breadth and depth of the calamity to Europe and America. Mr. Lincoln had come nobly through a great ordeal. He had extorted the approval even of his opponents. On this side of the water they had reluctantly come to admire his firmness, fairness, and sagacity."

The *Star* said:

"While the civilized world will lament the cruel death of Mr. Lincoln, now that the pro-slavery rebellion has been put down, and slavery received its death-blow, he has accomplished the mission he was raised to fulfill, and leaves behind a pure and spotless name—the name of a martyr as well as a patriot."

The London *Spectator* published an elaborate review of the character of Mr. Lincoln, from which the following paragraph is taken:

"We all remember the animated eulogium on Gen. Washington which Lord Macaulay passed, parenthetically, in his essay on Hampden: 'It was when, to the sullen tyranny of Laud and Charles, had succeeded the fierce conflict of sects and factions, ambitious of ascendency or

burning for revenge; it was when the vices and
ignorance which the old tyranny had engen-
dered, threatened the new freedom with destruction, that England missed the sobriety, the
self-command, the perfect soundness of judgment, the perfect rectitude of intention to which
the history of revolutions furnishes no parallel,
or furnishes a parallel in Washington alone.'
If that high eulogium was fully earned, as it
was, by the first great President of the United
States, we doubt if it has not been as well
earned by the Illinois peasant proprietor and
village 'lawyer,' whom, by some divine inspira-
tion of Providence, the Republican caucus of
1860 substituted for Mr. Seward as their nom-
inee for the President's chair."

The satirical London *Punch*, which had selected
its sharpest arrows for the ungainly emancipator
while living, came forward with its apology and
tribute, which is given below entire:

ABRAHAM LINCOLN,

FOULLY ASSASSINATED APRIL 14, 1865.

You lay a wreath on murdered Lincoln's bier—
　You, who with mocking pencil wont to trace,
Broad for the self-complacent British sneer,
　His length of shambling limb, his furrowed face;

His gaunt, gnarled hands, his unkempt, bristling hair;
　His garb uncouth, his bearing ill at ease;
His lack of all we prize as *debonair*,
　Of power or will to shine, of art to please;

You, whose smart pen backed up the pencil's laugh,
　Judging each step, as though the way were plain;
Reckless, so it could point its paragraph,
　Of chief's perplexity or people's pain.

Beside this corpse, that bears for winding-sheet
　The Stars and Stripes he lived to rear anew,
Between the mourners at his head and feet—
　Say, scurrile jester, is there room for you?

Yes, he had lived to shame me from my sneer,
　To tame my pencil and confute my pen;
To make me own this kind of princes' peer—
　This rail-splitter a true-born king of men.

My shallow judgment I had learned to rue,
　Noting how to occasion's height he rose;
How his quaint wit made home-truth seem more true;
　How, iron-like, his temper grew by blows.

How humble, yet how hopeful he could be;
　How in good fortune or ill the same;
Nor bitter in success, nor boastful he,
　Thirsty for gold nor feverish for fame.

He went about his work—such work as few
　Ever had laid on head, and heart, and hand—
As one who knows, Where there's a task to do,
　Man's honest will must Heaven's good grace command;

Who trusts the strength will with the burden grow,
   That God makes instruments to work his will,
If but that will we can arrive to know,
   Nor tamper with the weights of good and ill.

So he went forth to battle on the side
   That he felt clear was Liberty's and Right's,
As in his peasant boyhood he had plied
   His warfare with rude Nature's thwarting mights—

The uncleared forest, the unbroken soil;
   The iron-bark, that turns the lumberer's ax;
The rapids, that o'erbears the boatman's toil;
   The prairie, hiding the mazed wanderer's tracks;

The ambushed Indian, and the prowling bear—
   Such were the needs that helped his youth to train;
Rough culture, but such trees large fruit may bear,
   If but their stocks be of right girth and grain.

So he grew up a destined work to do,
   And lived to do it; four long suffering years
Ill-fate, ill-feeling, ill-report lived through,
   And then he heard the hisses change to cheers,

The taunts to tribute, the abuse to praise,
   And took both with the same unwavering mood;
Till, as he came on light from darkling days,
   And seemed to touch the goal from where he stood,

A felon hand, between the goal and him,
   Reached from behind his back, a trigger press'd—
And those perplexed and patient eyes were dim,
   Those gaunt, long laboring limbs were laid to rest!

The words of mercy were upon his lips,
　Forgiveness in his heart and on his pen,
When this vile murderer brought swift eclipse
　To thoughts of peace on earth, good-will to men.

The Old World and the New, from sea to sea,
　Utter one voice of sympathy and shame!
Sore heart, so stopped when it at last beat high!
　Sad life, cut short just as its triumph came!

A deed accursed! Strokes have been struck before
　By the assassin's hand, whereof men doubt
If more of horror or disgrace they bore;
　But thy foul crime, like Cain's, stands darkly out.

Vile hand, that brandest murder on a strife,
　Whate'er its grounds, stoutly and nobly striven;
And with the martyr's crown crownest a life
　With much to praise, little to be forgiven!

Young man, friend and brother, we have seen
what honesty, Christian principles, and persevering industry accomplished for an obscure pioneer
laborer. If we practice the same virtues, we can
not fail to win the confidence and affection of
our fellow-men, or fail in usefulness to ourselves,
our friends, and our country. If we avoid his
errors, we will also avoid many of his sorrows.
If we give our hearts to Jesus, we may fail of
the distinction achieved by him on earth, but we

will be crowned with honors before which the brightest earthly glory is as emptiness and vanity. Let us stand up for ourselves, our honor, our purity, our manhood. Let us defend justice, liberty, and human rights, at any cost, and at all hazards. Above all, let us stand firm for JESUS, who was not ashamed to die for us; firm in honoring him by obeying him and following his example; and may his mighty arm uphold us to the end!

ABRAHAM LINCOLN.

BY WILLIAM CULLEN BRYANT.

O, slow to smite and swift to spare!
 Gentle, and merciful, and just!
Who in the fear of God did'st bear
 The sword of power—a nation s trust—

In sorrow by thy bier we stand,
 Amid the awe that hushes all,
And speak the anguish of a land
 That shook with horror at thy fall.

Thy task is done—the bond are free;
 We bear thee to thy honored grave,
Whose proudest monuments shall be
 The broken fetters of the slave.

Pure was thy life; its bloody close
 Has placed thee with the sons of light,
Among the noble host of those
 Who perished in the cause of Right.

www.ingramcontent.com/pod-product-compliance
Lightning Source LLC
Chambersburg PA
CBHW032009060726
47497CB00017B/2424